A Cowboy Came With Fewer Complications Than A Man From The City....

Or so Carly thought. He ought to be easy to get along with. He didn't come with a lot of excess baggage. He rode his horse, drove a pickup truck while listening to country-western music, looked after his cattle and didn't worry about issues that plagued the rest of the world. The fantasy man had spun around in Carly's imagination for weeks.

But is that Hank? Carly frowned to herself. *Is he the fantasy cowboy I dreamed up?*

Maybe not, she reasoned. He wasn't a cardboard cutout of a man. He wasn't shallow and empty-headed.

He was real. He was smart and capable, not to mention definitely an accomplished lover....

Dear Reader,

This month Silhouette Desire brings you six brand-new, emotional and sensual novels by some of the bestselling— and most beloved—authors in the romance genre.
Cait London continues her hugely popular miniseries THE TALLCHIEFS with *The Seduction of Fiona Tallchief*, April's MAN OF THE MONTH. Next, Elizabeth Bevarly concludes her BLAME IT ON BOB series with *The Virgin and the Vagabond*. And when a socialite confesses her virginity to a cowboy, she just might be *Taken by a Texan*, in Lass Small's THE KEEPERS OF TEXAS miniseries.

Plus, we have Maureen Child's *Maternity Bride*, *The Cowboy and the Calendar Girl*, the last in the OPPOSITES ATTRACT series by Nancy Martin, and Kathryn Taylor's tale of domesticating an office-bound hunk in *Taming the Tycoon*.

I hope you enjoy all six of Silhouette Desire's selections this month—and every month!

Regards,

Melissa Senate

Senior Editor
Silhouette Books

Please address questions and book requests to:
Silhouette Reader Service
U.S.: 3010 Walden Ave., P.O. Box 1325, Buffalo, NY 14269
Canadian: P.O. Box 609, Fort Erie, Ont. L2A 5X3

NANCY MARTIN
THE COWBOY AND THE CALENDAR GIRL

SILHOUETTE *Desire*®

Published by Silhouette Books

America's Publisher of Contemporary Romance

THE COWBOY AND THE
CALENDAR GIRL

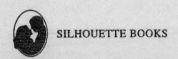 SILHOUETTE BOOKS

ISBN 0-373-76139-2

THE COWBOY AND THE CALENDAR GIRL

Copyright © 1998 by Nancy Martin

Printed in U.S.A.

NANCY MARTIN

has lived in a succession of small towns in Pennsylvania, though she loves to travel to find locations for romance novels in larger cities—in this country and abroad. Now she lives with her husband and two daughters in a house they've restored and are constantly tinkering with.

If Nancy's not sitting at her word processor with a stack of records on the stereo, you might find her cavorting with her children, skiing with her husband or relaxing by the pool. She loves writing romance fiction and has also written as Elissa Curry.

One

"Every woman falls for a cowboy at least once in her life," said Bert Detwiler, tossing the sheaf of black-and-white photos down on his immaculate black acrylic desk. "Looks like your number's up this time, Carly."

"Don't be ridiculous."

Carly Cortazzo blew cigarette smoke as she paced the tenth-floor office she shared with Bert, her partner at Twilight Calendars. In their slickly modern headquarters, Bert and Carly had created some of the bestselling provocative pinup calendars that ever graced America's gas stations, office water coolers and teacher lounges. But their success, Bert claimed, came from their mutual cold-bloodedness when it came to choosing the sexy photographs featured in Twilight's calendars.

Except Carly wasn't feeling very cold-blooded these days.

"I'm not going to fall for the guy," Carly insisted, trying to sound sincere. "I just think he's photogenic, that's all. Look at those sample shots again. He's dripping with sex appeal!"

Bert studied the photos once more, then raised his brows fastidiously and shot a piercing glance up at Carly. "He's dripping with sweat, dear."

"Well, sweat is always a hit with our customers—and the mustache and muscles don't hurt, either. And look at that horse! He's magnificent!"

"How Freudian," Bert observed coolly. "Look, it's too expensive to do location shoots. We've always agreed on that."

"Well, I think we need to spend the extra money. Our calendars are getting stale. If we're going to compete with Fabio and that basketball player with the purple hair, it's time we wowed our customers again."

"And you think this cowboy can do the wowing?"

"Absolutely. *If* we take the photos on his ranch with horses and that beautiful sky to counterpoint his look."

Bert bent closer to examine the photos. "He's not bad, I guess."

"Not bad! He's incredible!"

"I've never seen you so taken with someone." Bert glanced up at Carly, his eyes twinkling. "Should I be jealous?"

Carly sighed impatiently and hastily snatched up the top picture, the one she liked most. "Bert, you and I haven't been an item for three years."

Bert turned up the wattage on his smile. "Still, I get pangs now and then. You're looking terrific these days, Carly. I love the new haircut."

"It isn't new, Bert," she returned, automatically brushing the straight blond tendrils behind her ears. "But thanks for noticing."

"I notice more than you think." Bert put one elbow on his desk and leaned toward her. "Like how you've been feeling lately."

"What do you mean?"

"You *know* what I mean."

Carly turned away from her partner, lest he see her reaction. *Better to keep this relationship with Bert strictly professional,* she thought. After their mercifully short affair three years ago, Carly decided to keep her feelings to herself to insure Twilight Calendars continued to run successfully. Back then business had been far more important to Carly than a love life. But Bert had apparently picked up on her current state of mind.

It must have become obvious that Carly had recently begun to feel—well, jaded. Cynical. *The calendar business could have that effect on a girl. A few years of looking at every man in terms of how he'd photograph without his clothes on under some good studio lighting has turned me into just another L.A. vulture.*

She crushed out her cigarette with a vengeance in the cut-crystal ashtray on Bert's desk.

Looking at the mess she'd made in his ashtray, Bert said, "I think this cowboy thing has really affected you, Carly. You truly want to get this guy's shirt off, don't you?"

"Oh, that's not it at all!" Carly turned to the huge office window. Keeping her back to Bert, she frowned at the hazy panorama of Los Angeles. But she didn't really look at the familiar cityscape that stretched as far as the eye could see before disappearing into the smoggy horizon. Instead, Carly looked into her own heart for the first time in years.

"I've been doing this too long," she said aloud—before she could catch herself.

"What do you mean by that?" Bert sounded truly surprised.

Although she hadn't meant to reveal her innermost thoughts, Carly found herself confiding in Bert Detwiler of all people—her partner and former lover, who paid more attention to the care of his cashmere sweaters than the women in his life. But these days Bert was all Carly had.

Without turning around, Carly shook her head. "I've been obsessed with appearances, Bert. It's part of our job, of course—taking pictures that will titillate men and women everywhere—but, well, I've let it take over my personal life, too. The people I photograph are completely empty. Now they're the ones I socialize with, too. And they're not real."

"Oh, don't give me that beautiful-people-have-no-soul garbage again, Carly! We have rich social lives. Why, you're always running to some gallery opening or movie premiere or dinner with the gang—"

"And my biological clock is running, too."

"Good heavens." Bert clapped a hand over his heart as if to calm its lurching. "I never expected *you* to want a family. What an extraordinary idea."

Carly spun around and found Bert looking

amused. "All right, all right," she said wryly, indicating her spike heels, black stockings and black minidress. "So I'm not exactly an earth mother," Carly said. "But I see my sisters building wonderful lives with men who are interesting and talented, and what do I have to show for all my thirty-two years? Six shiny calendars featuring completely mindless guys who've smeared their pectorals with petroleum jelly!"

"You think this cowboy person has a soul?" Bert tapped the photo on his desk.

"At least he looks like he puts in an honest day's work that doesn't require false eyelashes and a chin tuck every five years the way most of our male models—"

"What *is* this?" Bert demanded with a laugh. "A midlife crisis?"

"I don't know what it is! I just looked at these pictures and saw a real person for the first time in ages."

"Okay, okay!" Bert used both hands to shove the rest of the jumbled photographs across the desk to her. "Take your camera and go to North Whatsit—"

"*South* Dakota."

"Whatever." He waved his hand dismissively. "If you really want to get a taste of a real man, forget the studio shots for once! Just remember…we need another bestseller this year, Carly."

"I'll remember," she said with a soft smile for her partner.

Bert's perfect grin twinkled again. "And one more thing. The front of the horse is the part that bites, and the back of the horse is the part that kicks."

"Bert—"

"I know," he said, nobly holding up one hand to prevent her from saying something that might embarrass them both. "Sometimes I'm a jerk, but once in a while I'm wonderful, right?"

Carly laughed. "See you next week."

Heading for the airport two hours later, Carly felt extraordinarily free. Suddenly she couldn't get to South Dakota fast enough.

Things were going to change!

One photograph had done it. Just one of the thousand amateurish pictures sent by fans of Twilight Calendars for the annual talent search. One Becky Fowler had submitted the winning photo—a picture of her own brother, a rancher with amazingly deep blue eyes, an awe-inspiring profile and—oh, well, she might as well admit it—gorgeous shoulders.

And ever since she'd laid eyes on that picture, Carly hadn't been able to think straight. All she wanted was to meet the man in the photo.

He looked like the kind of guy a girl could kiss until his cows came home.

He was magnificent. One photograph had captured this exquisite example of the male animal.

And his name was Hank, the letter said. Hank Fowler.

Hank. Perfect. Ever since seeing his picture, Carly had felt drawn to Hank Fowler as if by an unbelievably powerful magnet. Secretly she had started keeping his photo in her briefcase. At night she even put the picture on her nightstand. It was as if Hank called to some basic female instinct in Carly. And like a hormone-demented salmon swimming for the pool in which it was spawned, Carly suddenly knew she had to single-mindedly propel herself to the place where the handsome Hank Fowler lived and breathed.

And she didn't even *know* the guy.

But she wanted to meet him. A real man. Nothing artificial, nothing dishonest. The genuine article.

The plane deposited Carly in Sioux Falls. There she was informed that renting a car was her only choice for transportation, so she plunked down her gold credit card and acquired a four-by-four Jeep.

"I don't think you'll run into any snow," said the rental clerk. "It's pretty late for weather like that, but you never know."

"It's summer," Carly protested.

"You're in South Dakota now, honey. Anything can happen."

With a grin, Carly heard herself saying, "Oh, I hope so."

She drove a few hundred miles, occasionally looking at the map spread out on the passenger seat and muttering to herself when towns did not appear where they were supposed to. Within a few hours, much closer to her goal, she hoped, she ended up on a wide-open landscape with tall grass as far as the eye could see.

And then Carly saw him. She knew it was him.

Hank.

His first appearance was like something out of a movie finale.

On the horizon, the silhouette of a rearing horse lashed the setting sun. Then the horse landed on all

fours and bolted along the ridge with his rider clinging effortlessly to his rhythmic strides. They galloped
along the brilliant sunset-painted horizon—a thundering black stallion and the one man who could control him.

Carly could almost hear theme music.

She got out and leaned weakly against the hood
of the truck and watched, speechless. In her chest
she felt her heart start to thrum like a tuning fork
vibrating to an exquisite sound, as he turned and galloped straight toward her—a knight on his charger
swooping down to carry off a maiden.

Carly's knees actually began to tremble. She put
one hand to her forehead to shield her eyes from the
sun, and her mouth got very dry. But her gaze remained riveted on the man and horse bearing down
upon her with all the unstoppable power of a prairie
twister.

But he did stop. Inches from the Jeep, the horse
suddenly slid to a halt in a cloud of dust. And with
all the grace of a dancer, Hank Fowler flew down
from the saddle and landed on his feet just a yard
from where Carly stood.

Breathless, Carly stared into the bluest eyes she
had ever seen—crinkled at the corners, marked by
commanding dark brows, set deeply into a rugged
male face—the face she had memorized ever since
receiving his photograph. She couldn't breathe,
couldn't think.

"You...you're Hank Fowler," she gasped when
her brain kicked into gear.

"And who the hell," he said roughly, "are you?"

Carly still couldn't manage to verbalize a complete

thought. *He's gorgeous. He's everything I imagined. A real-life cowboy. I'm going to faint right here.*

He glared at her, holding his reins in one gloved hand. His jeans were snug and covered by a pair of leather chaps that looked incredibly sexy. Carly could imagine his calendar photo already—just the jeans and leather, no shirt. And those dusty boots— perfect! His hat looked thoroughly broken in by years of riding the range, too. He looked real—lean and mean and just dangerous enough to send a woman's hormones into a tailspin.

Belatedly, Carly stuck out her hand. "I...I'm Carly Cortazzo. It's great to meet you."

He used his teeth to yank off the glove on his right hand, then took Carly's in a bone-crushing grip. His blue eyes remained narrow, however. "Am I supposed to know you?"

Carly laughed, feeling like a starstruck basketball fan suddenly landing on the same planet with Michael Jordan. "Well, uh, not exactly, I guess. I just—you see, I'm from the calendar contest."

"The what?"

"Twilight Calendars. Surely you—I mean, your sister *did* tell you I was coming?"

His suspicious expression changed into a glare that was far more disturbing. "My sister Becky? What in tarnation has she gone and done now?"

For the first time since leaving L.A., Carly felt a twinge of consternation.

"You don't know?" she asked. "Nobody's told you about winning the contest?"

He lifted one menacing brow. "I'm betting it ain't like winning the lottery."

"Well, a little." Carly attempted to smile again, but suddenly found herself gulping in the presence of the man who had haunted her fantasies for several weeks now. *If he only knew what's been flitting around in my head....*

"Look," he said when she didn't continue. "I don't know what you're talking about, but you've just crossed onto Fowler land, and—"

"Oh, I'm not trespassing. I've been invited."

"You mean Becky's actually asked you to come onto the ranch?"

"Why, yes. To take your picture."

"To take my *picture?* What the hell for?"

"Our calendar."

He peered at her as if she were speaking a foreign language. "What kind of nonsense are you talking? You must have the wrong guy."

"Believe me, I don't. You're perfect, Mr. Fowler. I've never met anyone so naturally photogenic."

He squinted. "You calling me some kind of pretty boy?"

"Oh, no, of course not!" Carly said hastily. "Not exactly, that is. The camera does catch certain elements that might be unappreciated by the naked eye, so—"

His patience ran out and he interrupted her. "Look, I've got work to do. If you get this truck turned around, you'll find the main road in a couple of miles."

"But...but...I've already made all the arrangements with your sister to take your photograph."

"My sister," said Hank Fowler, "is not my keeper."

"But—"

"Forget it." He turned back to his horse.

Carly felt the beginnings of anger start to steam behind her eyelids. "Look, Mr. Fowler," she said, "I've communicated with your sister on this matter and I thought we'd reached an agreement. A ten-thousand-dollar agreement. Perhaps you'd better give me directions so that I can settle the details with her."

He tilted his hat and shot a measuring glance at Carly from beneath the brim. "Why don't you take a picture of yourself, Miss—what was your name?"

"Cortazzo. Carly Cortazzo."

"Right. Now, *your* picture might actually sell."

Carly felt herself flush. "Is that a compliment, Mr. Fowler?" It hadn't *felt* terribly complimentary.

With an easy swing, he climbed back into the saddle. An unsettling ghost of a grin flashed briefly across his rugged features as the magnificent horse danced beneath him. He put two fingers on the brim of his Stetson in a John Wayne salute before saying, "Take it any way you like, Miss Cortazzo."

"Where are you going?"

"Back to work."

"But...but...you can't leave like this!"

"Can't I?"

Carly gritted her teeth. "I...I...oh, hell." Throwing pride to the four winds, she said, "I'm lost! I've been wandering around these same three godforsaken counties all afternoon, and I'm darn sure I'll never find my way out of them without Sacajewea to guide me."

"All right, all right," he said, perhaps hiding a

grin. "Maybe you'd better not try driving back to town before dark. Something tells me you'll get worse than lost. Go up to the house."

"What house? I never saw a house."

He pointed. "Backtrack a mile. Take a right at the clump of pine trees, go two miles and you'll see the ranch. Becky's there. The two of you can wrangle this out."

"But you—"

"Get along, Miss Cortazzo," he growled, reining the horse around. "It'll be dark soon."

And he left her in a cloud of dust. With a gulp, Carly watched him go, forgetting her troubles. Dazzled by the glare of sunset and the vision of manhood that disappeared as magically as he'd come, she stared after him, entranced. Her heart pounded along with the rapid strides of the galloping horse.

"Wow," she breathed.

Thundering into the corral, Hank Fowler let out a whoop.

Of terror.

Then his horse jammed his forefeet into the ground, and Hank tumbled head over heels over the animal's head.

He landed in the dust at his sister's feet and lay stunned at the impact.

"You're a diaster!" Becky exclaimed, not moving from the spraddle-legged stance that was as natural to her as breathing. Becky was the real cowhand—the one who'd been born to run a ranch. When the horse reared over Hank's prone body, Becky grabbed the loose reins to keep the panting beast from trampling Hank into a million pieces.

"What the hell," she demanded, furiously glaring down at her brother, "do you think you're doing, Henry? Don't you know how valuable Thundercloud is?"

He spat dust from his mouth. "That stupid horse of yours ran away with me!"

"I *told* you. You have to show him who's boss!"

"I *tried!*" Hank cried, painfully sitting up on one elbow. "But you know how I hate horses, and they must be able to feel it! This isn't going to work, Beck."

"It *has* to work, Henry. I need the money!"

Gingerly Hank felt along his ribs to make sure none of them were broken. "I can't believe you talked me into this," he muttered. "I swore I'd never come back to this damned ranch as long as I live. And the charade you came up with gets more ridiculous by the minute! I'm just *not* a cowboy!"

Becky hunkered down on her heels and grinned at him. "But you're still going to help me, right? Look, we'll practice with Thundercloud all day tomorrow. I promise he won't run away with you again. By the time that lady from the calendar company gets here, you'll look like a *real* cowhand."

Wryly Hank shook his head. "There aren't enough years left in both our lifetimes to change me, Beck. Besides, she's on her way." Hank put his hand up for Becky to help him to his feet.

Her grip was firm and sure, and she hauled him up easily. "What do you mean?"

Suppressing a groan as his muscles protested,

Hank tried to brush some of the dust off his borrowed chaps. "I met her."

"You *met* her? What are you talking about?"

"This precious horse of yours practically dumped me in her lap. He tore over the hill and threw me as soon as we were out of your sight. By some miracle I landed on my feet. She was there."

"*Where?*" Becky demanded.

"Out on the south road. I gave her directions. She'll be here any minute."

"Any *minute?*" Becky cried. "You're kidding! Did she fall for it? You didn't mess things up, did you?"

"Don't worry. I kept the script simple."

"You talked? First you fell off the horse and then you talked? What did you say?"

"Nothing intelligent, I assure you. After this four-legged locomotive threw me I was a little rattled, so I improvised, that's all."

Becky groaned. "Oh, no. I thought I'd have at least a week to get you into shape!"

"A week or a month," Hank said with a grin. "It wouldn't help, Becky. I was never cut out for the cowboy life."

It was true. Even though he'd spent the first fifteen years of his life growing up on his parents' ranch deep in South Dakota, Henry Fowler was never meant to live anywhere but a few blocks from the nearest urban transit system. Despite his father's insistence that he learn to rope, ride and eat beans by a campfire out on the prairie, Henry Fowler had escaped the wide-open spaces for an East Coast prep school as soon as he had been able to get away.

After prep school had come four blessed years at Columbia University in New York, after which he'd bounced from one journalist job to the next—staying in each city only long enough to get his fill of the culture, the restaurants and the nearest climbing mountains. He'd made friends in every major city in the country and never once looked back on the life he might have had on the family homestead.

Until his sister, Becky, called with a crazy scheme.

"I think we'd better call it quits before she figures us out, Becky," Hank said, reaching for the borrowed Stetson that had rolled under the nearest fence rail. "Nobody's going to fall for me being a cowpoke."

"Don't say that!" Becky ordered, grabbing his elbow and steering Hank determinedly toward the barn. "We've got to make this work! If I don't get the money, I'll lose the ranch, Henry!"

"I thought you were supposed to call me Hank. You said it sounded tougher."

"It does," she agreed hastily. "Besides, if she's coming from Los Angeles, she might actually have heard of Henry Fowler."

"What do you mean 'might'?" Henry demanded. "My column is syndicated all up and down the West Coast. She'd have to be a hermit like you not to know who I am!"

Although he was based in Seattle now, Hank had begun to make a reasonably good living by writing his syndicated column—a few short paragraphs of weekly diatribe that resulted from the forays he made into the mountains with so-called celebrities. Mostly Hank invited local politicians on physically challenging outings and wrote about their reactions. His piece on a presidential hopeful had ruined the man's plan for a national campaign. Good thing, too. A man who threw trash on a mountain trail didn't deserve to be president of anything.

Over the past couple of years, Hank had begun to attract a loyal following, who now sent him more material than he could use. Every day he received a bucketload of letters that fulminated on subjects ranging from the logic of pasting brassiere advertisements on the sides of city buses to the latest political faux pas committed by an elected dunderhead. Hank used the material to create funny columns that newspaper readers loved.

"You're the perfect guy for this column," one of his former girlfriends had told him. "You hate everything but your precious mountains. And you're funny about it."

"I don't hate you," he'd said to her.

"Not yet," she predicted, and she'd been right. Soon thereafter, her habit of chewing gum during every waking moment had driven him to distraction.

Dragging her brother into the privacy of the barn, Becky began to coach him urgently. "All right, the best thing to do is the strong and silent act. Cowhands are always strong and silent."

"Aren't we perpetuating movie stereotypes?"

"Don't talk like that! You can't— Oh, just keep your mouth shut when she gets here, and—"

"Have you ever known me to keep my mouth shut?"

"You've got to try!"

"Listen, Beck, this woman can't be looking for

anything but a pretty face—or in my case, a beaten-up mug. She isn't going to care if I can ride a horse or swing on a flying trapeze! Trust me. I know these Hollywood types, and all they want is a square jaw to photograph. If she's so demented as to want mine—"

"She said she wanted a cowhand. For ten thousand dollars, we're going to give her a cowhand!" Becky pulled the huge black horse into a stall and proceeded to loop the reins around the hay rack. Then she moved to untie the saddle girth, saying, "Just behave yourself, all right? Can't you remember *anything* about ranch life?"

"I've spent the past twenty years trying to forget."

Becky sighed impatiently and shook her head. "I can't believe you're really my brother!"

Hank put his arm across his sister's narrow shoulders, finding them tense with emotion. "Hey, take it easy, Beck."

"This is important, dammit! I could lose this place. And it's my *home!*" Her blue eyes suddenly flashed with tears. "I really need the money, Henry."

"Cool down," Hank soothed, sorry he'd teased her. "I said I'd help, didn't I?"

Becky tried to focus on unfastening the saddle again. "It was a silly idea. I should never have asked you to come out here—"

"Hey, I had a few vacation days saved up. No problem. I'll just explain to this calendar lady that I'm not who she thinks I am. I'm sure she doesn't give a damn about my line of work."

"But she does! She wants a real person. She said so on the phone."

"I *am* a real person."

"I mean an authentic cattle rancher."

"It doesn't matter what I do. She'll still want to put my face on her silly little calendar, so—"

"It's not just your face, Henry," his sister interrupted.

"What?"

Slowly Becky said, "Maybe I should have told you the whole story before now, but I thought we had a few more days before she actually got here and started—"

Hank glowered at his sister. "What whole story?"

"This...this calendar thing," Becky said uncomfortably. "It's not just pictures of good-looking guys' faces. If that was the case, you wouldn't have made the finalists' list."

Hank felt his mouth go very dry. "What are you talking about?"

"All those years of climbing and racquetball have done you some good, big brother. She wants to take pictures of the whole package."

A pang of dread shot through him. "Hold it—"

"I sent a bunch of old photos to the contest. She said she liked your look. Your total look."

"But—"

"I know, I know, you're not as young as you used to be, and there's a little flab around your middle, but modern photography—"

Incensed, Hank interrupted, "There is no flab around my middle!"

"Great," said Becky. "Then you won't be afraid to take off your shirt."

"Now wait a minute!"

"Or your trousers."

"Just a *damn* minute!"

"I hear a truck." Becky frantically tugged Hank's bandanna askew and tilted his Stetson to the correct angle. "There's no time to give you a complete makeover. Can't you— Oh, don't you have some tobacco to chew, at least?"

She dashed out of the barn. Stunned by the information his conniving sister had just sprung on him, Hank stood frozen for a split second—just long enough for Thundercloud to reach around and sink his big yellow teeth into Hank's arm.

With a yelp, Hank leaped out of the stall and slammed the door behind him. He could swear he heard Thundercloud chuckle with satisfaction. Fuming, he followed his sister outside.

Becky was already outside, calling hello to someone.

"Hi. Miss Fowler?" asked a female voice.

"That's me," Becky replied. "You must be Miss Cortazzo from Los Angeles."

"Call me Carly."

Hank arrived at the open barn door in time to see his sister clasp hands with the slender young woman dressed almost entirely in black. Her white-blond hair was a dramatic counterpoint to the dark clothes, and her fair skin and pale blue eyes looked gorgeous in the fading sunlight.

"We weren't expecting you yet," Becky said.

"I'm sorry. My office was supposed to fax you."

"Oh, we don't have a fax machine."

"Well, I guess you really wouldn't need one out here," said Carly Cortazzo with a smile. She glanced around the barn and corral and let her gaze travel to the view of the Black Hills beyond. "This is beautiful country. I almost enjoyed getting lost in it."

"Hen—I mean, Hank says he gave you directions to the ranch. Maybe he should have led the way."

"Oh, I don't think Hank wants to get too friendly with me."

She turned and met his eyes with a wry smile playing at the corners of her mouth. Hank hadn't gotten a good look at her before. His terror of Becky's runaway horse had muddled his head. But now he had a chance to give her a thorough once-over, and he liked what he saw.

Carly Cortazzo had self-assurance in every sinew of her lean, athletic body. Her blue gaze was confident, and her clothing had a cosmopolitan flare of drama. Hank liked the way her light hair wisped around the sharp contours of her face and emphasized the slender grace of her long neck. She had a businesslike manner—belied only by the lush curve of her sensual lips that lent a vaguely vulnerable cast to her face.

She wasn't one of the fresh-scrubbed country girls Hank had grown up with in South Dakota, but had an energetic kind of beauty accompanied by a slight gleam of cynicism in her gaze.

He felt a shiver of excitement zap through his body as their gazes held and crackled with electricity.

Almost too late he remembered he was supposed to be a cowboy, so he lounged against the barn door and pulled his Stetson a little lower over his forehead.

"Nope," he drawled laconically, doing his best Wyatt Earp imitation. "I don't aim to get too friendly. Not just yet, anyway."

Carly raised one elegant eyebrow and seemed undaunted.

Becky cleared her throat noisily and gave Hank a what-the-hell-are-you-doing glare. Then she said, "How about if my brother takes your gear up to the guest room, Carly? I've got a horse to tend at the moment."

"Don't let me keep you from your work," Carly replied, still eyeing Hank with laserlike intensity. "I can take care of myself."

"Fine. Hank, will you—"

"Sure," said Hank, pushing off from the barn door and moseying over to the Jeep. He grabbed two large suitcases from the front seat. Together, they weighed almost as much as a Hereford steer, but Hank pretended he was accustomed to carrying much heavier loads as he hoisted the leather strap of one suitcase over his shoulder. "Think you packed enough duds, ma'am?"

"I wasn't sure what to expect," she retorted. "So I brought a little of everything."

"Always good to be prepared," he shot back in his best cowboy drawl. "You never know what might happen out in these parts."

Maybe his cowboy act wasn't as good as he'd hoped. He thought he heard Becky give a little moan of dismay as he led Carly Cortazzo toward the house.

Two

It was all Carly could do to keep from ogling Hank Fowler as he led her up the plank steps of his modest farmhouse. He had the nicest butt she'd ever seen encased in dusty blue jeans. And those leather chaps seemed to—well, she wanted to rip open one of her suitcases, get out her camera and start the test shots immediately.

"After you, ma'am," he said, pushing open the door and stepping back a pace.

"Thanks." Carly preceded him into the small house and hoped he hadn't guessed where her thoughts had lingered. She glanced around to get her bearings in the house.

The main room was humble, with heavy wooden beams supporting the ceiling, but it was cozily decorated with calico curtains at the windows, rough-hewn furniture scattered around a stone fireplace and a hand-carved checkers game set out on a low coffee table that was also strewn with magazines, enamel coffee cups and a well-used sewing basket.

Very homey, Carly thought. Very country. Frankly, she hated the look, going in for the uncluttered modern mode of decorating herself. But it was definitely...homey.

From the connecting room wafted the rich aroma of hot food slowly steaming on the stove. A multicolor braided rug lay on the floor, and a large woolly dog snoozed contentedly by the fire.

Upon their arrival, however, the dog got up and growled. He was the size of a small pony, with a ragged gray coat snarled with shaggy tufts that gave him the appearance of a huge porcupine that had been tumbled in a clothes dryer.

"Don't mind Charlie," said Hank, behind her. "He's too old to do any real damage."

"He looks like a wolf," Carly said, stopping in the middle of the room as the dog approached. Normally she liked dogs—the kind small enough to be carried in a woman's handbag at least. But this one looked as though he could swallow her arm for an appetizer.

"Half wolf," Hank explained. "He's my sister's idea of a pet."

The beast came closer and sniffed Carly suspiciously, still making a gurgling growl in the back of his throat. But his tail started to wag gently, so she risked patting his broad head. "Nice boy. Nice Charlie."

As Hank went past, Carly could have sworn the

dog started to growl again, but Hank didn't seem to take notice. He said, "Don't worry. Charlie only bites if he's hungry."

"Are you trying to scare me into leaving, Mr. Fowler?"

He turned and grinned. It was a devastating smile, complete with crinkled eyes that glinted appealingly. "Would it work if I tried?"

"Not likely. I'd like to stay and give your sister ten thousand dollars."

"In exchange for my picture, you mean."

"I think it's a fair deal."

Hank unslung the suitcase he'd been carrying and braced one shoulder casually against a timbered beam. Leaning there, he looked almost too big for the room—like a man who belonged in the wide-open spaces instead of a little house cluttered with countrified knickknacks. Carly might have felt small and insignificant—if she hadn't seen the gleam of mutual attraction in his blue gaze.

He said, "There must be guys who are really worth that much money. But me—I'm just ordinary."

"Ordinary can be nice."

"I hate looking silly."

"The photo doesn't have to be silly."

The amusement in his gaze sparkled. "I've seen the particular kind of calendars you make, ma'am. And they look mighty silly to me."

"They make money. A lot of money."

"Money's not the most important thing in the world."

"It seems pretty important to your sister," Carly

reminded him. "Are you going to disappoint her because you're afraid to let yourself look foolish?"

"But—" he shook his head as if confounded "—why me, Miss Cortazzo?"

"Why *not* you?"

"There's nothing special about me!"

"You're wrong."

Carly almost told him the truth then. About her daydreams and nighttime fantasies ever since laying eyes on his photograph. There *was* something special about Hank Fowler—something that spoke to the deepest part of Carly's soul. Maybe not every woman would see him the same way, but she knew she had the right man to use to create an object of desire. A lot of women were going to pay money to admire Hank Fowler. He was good-looking. He had a strong, lean, tensile kind of body that could seduce a camera.

Better yet, there was something in his gaze that few men possessed. It was magnetism and intelligence and humor and—oh, hell, Carly wasn't sure exactly what else. She only knew that looking into his eyes made her feel sexy.

"You're the right guy for this contest," she said finally. "You have the look that our marketing department wants most."

"Marketing department?" he said doubtfully. "You actually pay people to decide what kind of pictures go on those calendars of yours?"

Carly hesitated to reveal that the marketing department was made up of herself and Bert—just like nearly every other department at Twilight Calendars. But it sounded good.

She went on. "Our marketing department has been

very successful in the past. We manufacture one of the bestselling products in the country. We know what we want. And we want you, Mr. Fowler. We want a cowboy who can handle a horse, ride the range, shoot a gun—''

''Oh,'' he said with a grin. ''For a while there, I was afraid I was going to have to take my clothes off.''

''That wouldn't hurt, either.''

He blinked, startled. ''Do you have any idea how cold it gets out in this godforsak—I mean, out here in God's country? A guy would have to be nuts to take off his shirt and go riding around—''

''Our calendars are fantasies, Mr. Fowler. They're not supposed to portray real life.''

''Fantasies,'' Hank repeated.

He had a few fantasies starting in his own head at that moment.

Carly Cortazzo was the sort of woman he'd spent most of his adult life avoiding—smart, opinionated, ambitious and assertive. Probably temperamental, too. Mostly, Hank preferred to keep the company of beautiful but soft-willed women who let him dominate the relationship. It was immature of him, he knew, but it was easier to be the boss, he'd decided long ago. With the right partner, he got to do the things he enjoyed most and have the added benefit of a beautiful companion, too.

But Carly was a challenge. He guessed that starting a relationship with her would be like setting off a boxful of fireworks in a closed room. Just watching her tight, erect posture as she confronted him made Hank think of hot, passionate arguments. She was unpredictable and could probably do a lot of damage, if she chose.

He found himself fantasizing how explosive she might be in bed, too.

"Mr. Fowler?"

Hank yanked his attention back to the present and gave her a grin. "Sorry. What did you say?"

She controlled her patience with an obvious effort. "I asked if you have any objections to taking off your clothes for the calendar."

Hank nearly choked. "Hell, I haven't agreed to do it with my clothes *on,* let alone—"

"But your sister needs the money."

True, Hank thought, suppressing a groan.

For some insane reason he would never fathom, Becky had tied her heart and soul to the Fowler cattle ranch, and she needed a miracle to save the place from bankruptcy. A few years of low beef prices, hard winters and the high cost of feed had driven Becky to desperation. Of course Hank had pitched in his savings to help his sister, but eventually his own finances had run painfully dry. They needed a miracle, all right.

Unfortunately, Hank hadn't foreseen the miracle requiring him climbing into cowboy duds just to have them stripped off for a camera-toting beauty with a kissable red mouth and blue, bedroom eyes.

"Look, Miss Cortazzo," he began firmly, "I guess I have to go through with having my picture taken because my sister gave you her word, but wild horses won't get me out of my jeans."

She pounced. "How about your shirt?"

"No."

"But—"

"Absolutely not." Thoughts of his fellow journalists catching a glimpse of his photographed face had been hard enough to imagine. But if his colleagues got hold of anything more risqué, Hank knew he would be getting blackmail notes for the rest of his life. "No way, Miss Cortazzo."

She tried a more subtle approach. "I was thinking we could try some shots of you chopping wood. You might actually do that without a shirt, right?"

"I don't think so."

"How about—"

"There's no way I'm taking off anything."

He was saved from further arguments as they were interrupted at that moment by rushed footsteps on the porch. A moment later Becky burst into the house, breathless and flushed.

"Hen—I mean, Hank! Doc Vickery just stopped by. He says there's a buyer coming from out East who wants to look at our stock!"

"Great," said Hank, although he had no idea what in the world his sister was talking about.

Becky must have understood his meaningful glare, because she glanced toward Carly Cortazzo and explained—as if for the benefit of a newcomer, "That means we've got to have a roundup. You know, to gather up all the cattle and pen them here at the ranch for inspection."

"How exciting."

How awful, Hank almost said aloud. "What about Fred? Didn't you just give him a few days of vacation?"

"Who's Fred?" Carly asked.

"My—our hired hand," Becky replied, already headed for the telephone. "He helps around the ranch. I better call him right away. I can't round up all the cattle by myself."

"What about Hank?" Carly asked innocently. "Can't he help?"

Becky stumbled just as she reached the telephone, but Hank was glad to see she managed not to howl with laughter at the idea of her brother actually performing cowboy work. "Hank? Oh...sure. He'll help. Won't you, Hank?"

"Of course," Hank said, hoping he hadn't turned white at the thought of galloping all over the ranch in search of runaway cows.

"This will be great," Carly said with a big smile. "A real roundup! Maybe I'll get some good action shots—preliminary ideas to give to our photographer when she gets here."

Hank swallowed hard. "Uh, Becky, how about if I show Miss Cortazzo to the guest room, then you and I can talk this over?"

"Good idea," Becky said. "I'll call Fred while you take her upstairs."

Hank picked up Carly's luggage again. "This way, Miss Cortazzo."

He led the way up the narrow steps to the cramped second floor of the house. There was no hallway at the top—just a landing with four doors leading into the three small bedrooms and the bath. Hank shouldered open the door to the smallest of the three bedrooms.

And he promptly whacked his head on the low-hanging dormer. He staggered in pain, and smothered a curse.

"Are you all right?" Carly asked, right behind him.

"Yeah, sure."

Manfully pulling himself together, Hank tossed her luggage onto the single bed that was tucked under the eaves. He hoped she hadn't guessed that he hit his head because he'd forgotten the layout of the house he'd grown up hating.

Carly strolled to the bed and glanced around the small bedroom that Becky had carefully aired out and decorated with a watering can full of wildflowers. "How…quaint."

"Well, it's home," Hank said, for lack of anything more imaginative. His head was still spinning from the crack he'd taken on the dormer. Or maybe it was the heady perfume Carly wore that made him slightly dizzy. The scent was intoxicating. "Make yourself comfortable."

"Thank you."

"The window props open if you like fresh air at night."

"What an novel idea."

"No fresh air where you live?"

"In Los Angeles? We have smog, not air."

"I see. Well, the bathroom's the door opposite."

"Thanks." She turned away from the window and stood facing Hank just eighteen inches away in the small room. "I'd like to fix my makeup before dinner."

For a moment Hank forgot about risking his life in a roundup. Carly had the pale, peaches-and-cream skin of a pampered English lady—unusual for a California native. That creamy skin stretched down an elegantly long throat and plunged to the softly rounded curves of her breasts. Hank thought about tracing the line of her throat with his thumb just to test the delicacy of her skin, but banished the idea in favor of an indirect compliment instead. "You won't need makeup out here, Miss Cortazzo."

She heard the double meaning laced in his murmur and slanted a wry smile up at him. "I need makeup no matter where I am, Mr. Fowler. It's my link to civilization."

He laughed. He liked her, and decided it was safer not to discuss civilization. "Supper's ready when you are."

"I'll be down in a few minutes."

Hank lingered another moment, inhaling her fragrance, enjoying the light in her eyes and wondering what made her so damn tempting. She was good-looking and clever—a combination he enjoyed very much.

He hoped to hell she wasn't so clever that she'd see through his masquerade too quickly.

Remembering to keep up appearances, Hank tipped his hat and drawled, "Welcome to the Fowler ranch, ma'am. I hope you enjoy your stay."

"I'm sure I will."

Then he left the bedroom and thumped down the steps. Charlie growled at him. Hank growled back, then hurried to the kitchen. He cornered his sister there. Becky was just hanging up the phone as he arrived.

In a hushed whisper he demanded, ''What the hell have you gotten me into, Becky?''

''I'm sorry!'' Becky hissed back, trying to keep her voice down so they wouldn't be heard from upstairs. ''How was I supposed to know a buyer was coming this week?''

''When's he coming?''

''Day after tomorrow. We only have one day to round up all the cattle.''

''Did you get in touch with Fred?''

''He already left for his vacation in Disney World!''

''Then who—'' Hank saw the expression on his sister's face and felt the cold claw of dread grab his heart. ''I can barely sit on a horse, let alone get it to do anything but run away with me! You've got to find somebody else to help, Beck.''

Becky folded her arms over her chest and leaned back against a shelf full of preserved peaches. ''It's going to look awfully suspicious to the calendar lady if you don't saddle up and work the ranch, cowboy.''

''Then we need to come up with a plan—a logical reason why I'm not trying to get myself killed in a stampede.''

''You're not as bad at ranch work as you think you are,'' Becky soothed. ''Heavens, you were riding before you were three years old!''

''And getting thrown off every pony within five hundred miles. I *hate* horses, Becky, and they *know* I hate them. Now it's a conspiracy thing with the whole species.''

''We can't tell the calendar lady who you really

are. She specifically wants a cowboy, and we don't get the money unless you come through."

"Maybe I could break my leg or something. That would keep me out of harm's way."

Becky shook her head and frowned. "Too wimpy."

"Wimpy! A real cowhand would work with broken bones, is that it?"

"Probably. Think of something else."

He groaned. "Like what?"

Becky snapped her fingers. "I've got it. I'll send you to look for strays! All you have to do is leave the ranch and stay gone for the whole day."

"Where?"

"Anywhere! You can ride over the nearest hill, take a paperback book out of your saddlebag and read while the rest of us break our backs!"

"What happens if the horse runs away with me again?" Hank grinned as Becky blew an exasperated sigh. "Okay, okay, I can manage to stay in the saddle for a few hundred yards, I guess."

"Good. The alternative would be to distract the calendar lady."

"Distract her?"

Dryly, Becky added, "Of course, that wouldn't be too hard, by the looks of things."

"What are you talking about?"

"The two of you can't take your eyes off each other."

"Don't be ridiculous!" Hank prided himself on his ability to resist women when the situation merited.

Becky looked delighted at having annoyed him. "Your tongues are practically hanging out."

"Not true!" Hank flushed, hating the idea that he'd been so obvious.

Becky breezed out of the pantry and started to work on supper. "And she thinks you're the sexiest thing since colored underwear."

Hank followed his sister into the kitchen and couldn't help asking, "You think so?"

Becky took a container of premixed biscuits out of the refrigerator, cracked it open and proceeded to line the biscuits up on a cookie sheet. "Believe me, big brother, you could distract Miss Cortazzo with one hand tied behind your back."

Hank considered the situation. Yep, there was something exciting happening between himself and Carly Cortazzo. He found her very attractive. And according to Becky, the feeling might be mutual.

Trouble was, as far as Carly was concerned, Hank was supposed to be a tough cowboy.

Hank, however, preferred to live within walking distance of a subway system, fine restaurants, a good newsstand and at least one modern art museum. But every week he got out of the city to climb. Rock climbing was his passion. Fresh air, rock and ice. Those elements kept him sane. He wasn't a trail-mix kind of guy, of course. No, he could appreciate fine dining. But now and then he needed to test himself. Hacking out a foothold in any icy cliff made him feel alive.

Hank shook his head. "If I get close to her, she's going to see I'm no cowpoke."

"How do you know?"

"Because she's smart, dammit! Any fool can see I'm not Roy Rogers!"

Becky slid the tray of biscuits into the oven and bumped the door closed with her hip. "Did you get a look at her clothes?"

"Well, sure. They looked great."

"That's just it. She's dressed to *look* good. Even *you* knew enough to bring your oldest, warmest clothes out here. She's a complete dude!"

"Surely she'll see through me."

"Maybe you'll have time to cloud her vision before she sees too much."

"Meaning?"

"Meaning," Becky said, lifting the lid on the stew pot and giving the contents a quick stir, "you ought to take her out to the hay barn and see what develops."

"My allergy to hay?"

Becky laughed and replaced the lid on the pot. "You're determined to despise this place, aren't you?"

Putting his arm around Becky, Hank said fondly, "I just know I don't belong here, Beck." Looking down into his sister's tight expression, he felt his heart soften. "But you do, so let's do everything we can to keep the old family homestead."

Becky gave him a kiss on the cheek. "Thanks, Henry."

"Call me Hank. I'm starting to like it."

Becky laughed and punched his shoulder.

Dinner was ready by the time Carly came downstairs with her makeup freshly applied and a red bandanna around her throat just to get into the spirit of things.

"Dinner smells delicious."

"It's beef stew," Becky said proudly, busy at the stove with plates and a ladle. "I grew the vegetables myself."

"Not to mention the beef," Hank added. "And the herbs are better than ever this year."

"Herbs?" Carly asked.

Becky said, "Hank planned the herb garden himself, and his suggestions for seasonings are—well—uh—"

Hank opened the refrigerator. "Beer, anyone?"

"Why not?" Carly asked, wondering why Becky had faltered. She accepted a steaming plate of biscuits and stew from her as Hank got out the beer. There was enough food on Carly's plate to feed an entire family in L.A.

Becky prepared another plate for her brother. "I've got some phone calls to make if I'm going to round up enough men to help tomorrow. You two mind eating without me?"

"Not at all," Carly said, secretly pleased to have Hank all to herself for a while.

Hank seemed to hesitate for a split second. "You have to eat, Becky."

"I will," his sister promised. "In a few minutes. You go ahead. Entertain Carly for a while, all right? Tell her some stories about life on the ranch, why don't you? I'm sure she'd be interested in— Ouch!"

"Did I step on your foot?" Hank asked innocently. "Sorry, sis. This way, Miss Cortazzo. Let's eat on the porch, shall we?"

Carrying her plate, a bottle of beer and a napkin that Becky had thrust into the crook of her elbow, Carly followed Hank through the house and out onto the front porch. Besides two wooden rocking chairs and a porch swing suspended by chains from the rafters, there was a small painted table placed in one corner between a couple of old wicker chairs. Someone had already set the table with silverware and plaid place mats. A flickering yellow candle in a jar made the table look surprisingly romantic.

"Alfresco," Carly said. "How nice to be dining outside tonight."

"Unless the mosquitoes show up. Have a seat."

"Thank you." Carly set her plate on the table and made herself comfortable in the wicker chair. Then she noticed Hank wasn't following her example. He stood over her, as if undecided about joining Carly at all. She smiled up at him, one eyebrow raised. "I hope you don't feel as if you're having dinner with the enemy."

"The enemy?"

"Me." She gestured for him to sit down, which he finally did. "I'm your enemy because I'm pushing you to pose for my calendar."

"Trust me. If you were really my enemy, we wouldn't be so civilized, Miss Cortazzo."

"Carly," she corrected automatically, picking up a fork. "I detect a chill in the air, nevertheless. Or don't you go for city girls?"

"I go for all kinds of girls," he retorted, slugging his beer as if to steel himself for a difficult conversation.

"All kinds of girls? Care to tell me about some of them?"

He regarded her warily over the glowing candle. "Well, we don't get many unattached women in these parts."

"What about attached ones?"

"Married women? No, I don't go in for that stuff. Too messy. I like to get in and out of relationships as cleanly as possible."

"I gather you don't go in for the lasting kind of relationships, either." Carly sampled the stew and found it warm and savory.

"I haven't been lucky in love."

"You certainly are the quintessential cowboy."

"What's that supposed to mean?"

Carly glanced up, surprised by the heat in his voice. "Why, nothing really. You must fall in love with horses, not women."

He snorted. "That's a laugh."

"Then you *do* have a girlfriend?"

"Look, I don't know why we're talking about me," he began irritably, looking surprisingly uncomfortable.

"I like to get to know my subjects, that's all."

He leveled her a suspicious stare. "Really?"

Carly sipped from her own beer bottle to give herself time to think. "To tell the truth, no. But you— well, I've never met a real cowboy before. I just—I want to know what your life's like. Call it professional curiosity. For example, do you and your sister run this ranch all by yourselves?"

"Um, well, we have a hired hand, of course, to

help out. But usually, it's just a one—er, two-person operation.''

"That must mean a lot of hard work.''

He shrugged. "If you love it, it's not really work.''

"You love it, then?''

He took a huge forkful of stew into his mouth and took forever to chew it. "This stew is great, isn't it?'' he asked, after swallowing.

"Yes, it's delicious.''

"Becky has been adjusting the recipe again. I like the sage. And not too much onion.'' He thoughtfully selected a carrot with his fork. "The touch of jalapeño is just right. Not overwhelming, but definitely a statement.''

Delighted, Carly laughed. "You're a cowboy foodie!''

He looked up at her as if startled out of his thoughts. "A foodie?''

"Someone who appreciates good food.''

He bristled. "I'm not a gourmet. I hate pretentious stuff—''

"Like snooty French restaurants?''

"I do like French cuisine,'' he said cautiously, "if it's done well. But not an overly rich menu and a wine list that's past its prime.''

"Provençal food, though?''

He nodded. "Simple, but elegant.''

Carly leaned forward, glad to see him relaxing at last. "What's the best restaurant you've ever visited?''

Hank hesitated only for an instant. "There's a diner in Cheyenne that's top-notch. The best home-made sausage this side of the Mississippi." He looked cautious again. "Why are you asking?"

"No special reason. Conversation, I guess. And I like food myself. I keep a scrapbook of my favorite restaurants."

He looked surprised. "Yeah? What's in the scrapbook?"

"Well, I'm not exactly an expert," Carly admitted modestly. "I enjoy atmosphere as much as the food. I like to travel, so I've collected menus from restaurants in other countries. There's a small café in Vienna I loved—it just dripped with Italian color. But for food, I'd have to say a wonderful Chinese restaurant in Mexico City of all places—"

"Don Ho's!"

Carly couldn't hide her astonishment. "You've been there?"

Hank suddenly began to choke and reached for his bottle of beer. After a calming swallow, he shook his head. "Uh, no, I've never been there. I must have read about it in a magazine, I guess."

Carly studied him for a moment. "I don't suppose there are many restaurants around here."

"Not many, no."

"You're lucky Becky cooks so well."

"Becky's very talented," he agreed. "Of course, during the winters here she has lots of time to practice. She loves it, though."

Carly rested both her elbows on the table and leaned toward him. "Tell me what you love to do."

"Me?"

"Sure. What keeps you here at this ranch?"

"Um, well, the horses are—they're exciting, I guess."

"Exciting?"

"And cows. I've always...liked cows." *Preferably medium rare*, Hank almost added. He had begun to sweat beneath his flannel shirt.

"I see," Carly said, looking puzzled.

You're about to crash and burn, Hank thought to himself. *The whole restaurant discussion nearly gave you away. Now you just sound like an idiot.*

Determined to change the subject before he got into big trouble, he said, "Why are we talking about me again?"

Carly blinked at him over the flickering candle, her brows knit delicately. She appeared to be wrestling with exactly who the man across the table from her was.

Suddenly Hank could hardly choke down his food. His insides were knotted with tension. How was he supposed to keep up this charade?

I hate this ranch, he wanted to blurt out. *Give me a dirty old city with a few coffee shops, a good barber and tickets to an occasional basketball game, and I'll be happy as a clam. Let me climb Mount McKinley—just don't make me talk about ranching anymore.*

He couldn't tell the truth, though. Not until the damned photographs were snapped and printed in some ridiculous calendar that Hank could only pray never found its way into the sight of anyone he knew.

Obviously, however, he wasn't good at lying about the Fowler ranch. He had to come up with something else to talk about.

What had Becky advised? A distraction. Frantically, he remembered, *Maybe you'll have time to cloud her vision before she sees too much.*

He leaned on one elbow and said, "Why don't we talk about you, Carly."

"Me?"

"Sure. What are you really after when you chase down men and take their pictures?"

To Hank's immediate satisfaction, Carly Cortazzo blushed.

"I...it's my job, that's all."

"Your chosen profession," he reminded her. "You must enjoy what you do."

"Well, I—"

He met her uncertain gaze and held it with a long, slow smolder that caused Carly to gulp. *Aha, you've got her on the run.*

"Tell me, Carly," Hank went on, deepening his voice with shameless seductiveness. "Who's the sexiest man you've ever photographed?"

Her stunned expression told Hank that she definitely hadn't planned on having the tables turned.

"Well, they're not necessarily sexy to me," she finally blurted out.

"Surely one of them stands out in your mind, though?" he asked.

"Not one in particular, no."

"Are you saying you're impervious to the men you photograph for calendars?"

"Of course not," she said quickly, bristling at his unspoken suggestion that she didn't care for men at all. "They're usually not my type, that's all."

"What is your type?"

Fortunately for Carly their conversation was interrupted at that moment by a distant howl that sounded far off in the darkness. The eerie cry broke the still night with nerve-shattering results.

Carly jumped and looked out into the darkness beyond the porch. "What was that?"

"I haven't got the faintest—I mean, it was probably a wolf."

"A wolf!"

"Sure, we get them around here once in a while."

Her blue eyes were very wide as she stared into the dark night. "Are they dangerous?"

"Sure," Hank drawled. "All wolves are dangerous."

"Even lone wolves like you?" she asked, turning to gaze directly into his eyes.

"I'm not a loner—not exactly."

"But you keep things simple where women are concerned."

"Simple has its advantages," Hank replied with a smile.

Three

———

Fresh air gave Carly headaches. At least, that's what she told herself when she awoke the next morning and decided that a twinge in her forehead was probably the first sign of a major thumper.

Certainly her headache had nothing to do with a poor night's sleep thanks to an overactive imagination.

Dreaming about cowboys and wild horses hadn't given Carly her usual night's rest. She had tossed and turned for hours, sweating profusely when she woke up with thoughts of Hank Fowler dancing in her unconscious mind. She had envisioned him strolling into her bedroom, scooping her up out of the covers and striding off into the wilderness with her naked body in his strong arms. After all, isn't that what cowboys did with their women?

"He's gorgeous," she murmured to herself on a sigh, snuggling contentedly into the bedclothes. Those shoulders, that delicious mustache and his smoldery blue eyes!

Last night they'd talked for more than an hour on the porch, listening to the lone wolf howling in the distance. By candlelight, Hank's rough-hewn features had looked as devastating as any Hollywood hunk's, and Carly had gone to bed more infatuated than ever.

After that, her subconscious took over, and the resulting dreams had been deliciously erotic.

Too bad Hank hadn't tried to kiss her last night.

If he had, Carly might have hog-tied the man and dragged him up to her bed.

But no such luck.

The fragrance of hot coffee penetrated Carly's fogged brain at last, and she crawled out of the bed to check her wristwatch. Nine-thirty, California time. She had no clue what time it was in South Dakota, but the sun that streamed through the thin calico curtains seemed dazzlingly bright.

Groping on the nightstand, Carly discovered that her last pack of cigarettes was still empty. "Oh, damn."

She fell back into the pillows and groaned. "Why did I come all the way out here just to frustrate myself? It's obvious Hank Fowler thinks more about his horse than women—and now—no cigarettes!"

Grumbling, Carly climbed out of her bed and into her ancient pair of faded blue jeans. She added sneakers and a crisp white shirt purchased at an exorbitant price from a Western-style shop on Rodeo

Drive. She fluffed her hair in the bathroom mirror and applied a light version of her usual cosmetic routine before grabbing a sweater and descending the narrow staircase of the Fowler house.

Today she left her red bandanna upstairs. She had a feeling it looked silly.

In the kitchen she found a note propped by the coffeepot. "If you're awake before noon, join us outside."

Smart mouth.

The note was signed in an illegible, but unmistakably confident scrawl that Carly assumed was Hank's mark.

"If I'm awake before noon," she muttered grumpily, her pride stung. "What's he trying to do? Challenge me to get up with the chickens?"

She poured a mug of coffee for herself and made a cursory search of the various kitchen drawers in hopes that the clean-living Fowler family might have stashed some cigarettes someplace. No luck. With a sigh she strolled out onto the porch to sip her coffee.

The sunlight was so blazingly clear that she fumbled in her shirt pocket for her sunglasses and put them on. The coffee, thick and strong, evaporated her headache at once.

The ranch was a hive of activity. Carly could see Becky riding a large black horse around the corral, separating cows that fled before her like frightened wrens. A handful of men stood around a battered horse trailer, laughing as they unloaded their saddled horses. Clearly, they had been hired for a hard day's work, and they didn't mind a bit.

Hank detached himself from the group of men and sauntered across the dusty yard to Carly.

"'Morning," he drawled, coming to a halt and propping one boot on the bottom porch step. He was a vision of manliness in jeans and a red flannel shirt under a tight-fitting denim jacket. His gaze was clear beneath the brim of his hat. "You finally decide to join the land of the living?"

"I have a touch of jet lag," she replied, trying to sound calm despite the sudden acceleration in her pulse. The man was just as gorgeous by daylight as he had been the night before. The morning sun filled his blue eyes with a devilish gleam, and the rough denim jacket clung to his broad shoulders like a second skin.

"Sleep well?" he asked.

Had he guessed the subject of her dreams by the guilty flush that rose to her cheeks? Carly hoped not. "Yes, very well," she lied. "How about you, Mr. Fowler?"

"I think you could call me Hank by now. And we've known each other almost a whole day, right, Carly?"

She liked the way he said her name—half teasing, half caressing. "Right," she said briskly. "And we're going to get to know each other much better before it's all over, Hank. I just need a few minutes to load my cameras, then we can get started on the test shots for—"

"Sorry. Today's a bad day for me. As you can see, we've got a lot of work to do."

Carly tried to hide her disappointment, then heard herself asking rashly, "Is there anything I can do?"

"You know anything about cattle?"

"I prefer filet mignon to strip steaks, if that's what you mean."

With a laugh he said, "But can you ride a horse?"

"Of course." Then, realizing she might have just put her life in danger, Carly added slowly, "That is, if the real thing's not too different from a carousel ride."

Amused, Hank motioned her down the steps, then strolled beside Carly as they headed toward the corral. "It's not very different, as a matter of fact. You just sit still and enjoy the rhythm."

"Sounds easy enough," she said lightly, wondering if he had a double entendre in mind. "Do you have a nice, quiet horse I could try?"

"You're serious?"

Carly tossed caution to the winds. "Why not?"

"I wouldn't want you to get hurt."

"Oh, I'm tougher than I look," she assured him. "I'd like to help today. Really, I would."

"But—"

At that moment Becky rode up to the fence and reined her sweating horse to a stop. It was the same stallion Hank had been riding when he'd first appeared before Carly. A cloud of dust rose up and nearly engulfed Carly. She heard Hank cough.

"Hi," said a perky-sounding Becky. "Sorry we can't do the photos today, Carly."

"No problem."

Effortlessly Becky controlled her horse, which proceeded to snort and lunge against the reins. "Did I overhear you say you'd like to help today?"

"I'd love it!" Carly said.

Actually, she couldn't imagine gallivanting around on a horse in all this dreadful dust and fresh air, but Carly didn't want to let Hank Fowler out of her sight, now that she'd finally laid eyes on him.

Brightly she suggested, "Maybe Hank could look after me so I don't cause any trouble?"

"Sure," Becky answered, then suddenly faltered. "I mean—well, Hank's going to ride out to look for strays today. Maybe you'd better stick around the corral just to—"

"Oh, I'd love to go looking for strays!"

"But—" Becky and Hank began almost in unison.

"Oh, I'll be perfectly safe," Carly interrupted before either of them could voice their objections. "Hank can take care of me, right?"

"Well," Becky said, hesitantly glancing at her brother.

"I don't know." Hank exchanged looks with Becky. "I'm going to be pretty busy today."

"I'll stay out of trouble," Carly pleaded. "You won't even know I'm around. Please? Can't I go with you?"

"Why not?" Becky asked. She gave her brother a meaningful stare. "I've hired a few other guys to help out. We can handle things around here, I guess. Take a picnic, Hank. It might be fun."

"But—"

"Go on. Show Carly around the old homestead you love so much."

Hank felt panic rising up around his ears. Suddenly he wanted to strangle his sister. "But, Becky…"

"The boys and I can handle things around here. You go up into the hills and see what turns up."

"Sounds wonderful!" Carly cried, looking as starry-eyed as any city-bred greenhorn on her first day at the dude ranch. "I'll go see about a picnic, if you'll find me a suitable horse, Hank."

"Perfect plan," Becky said, looking pleased with herself.

Hank watched Carly turn and jog toward the house, and his dismay faded. Her beautifully curved backside looked great in jeans.

Maybe spending the day with her wasn't such a bad idea after all.

Becky leaned down from the saddle to murmur in her brother's ear. "It'll be fun. I promise. Besides, she'll just be in the way around here today."

"Don't try to make it sound like you're looking out for her safety," Hank growled. "You're just getting me deeper and deeper into trouble—and you're enjoying it!"

"I think you're going to like this kind of trouble," Becky predicted. "C'mon. I'll find you some gear and a couple of horses."

"A couple of ancient ones, please," Hank said, following his sister.

Half an hour later, Hank found himself holding the reins of two animals that had been humanely retired to the Fowler ranch after long lives cutting cattle elsewhere. Becky had a soft heart for old horses— no doubt one of the reasons why her finances were always such a mess.

"This one's Laverne," Becky said, patting the

speckled neck of a sad-looking Appaloosa. "And this one's Buttercup. Which one do you want?"

"They both look like they're on their last legs."

"Oh, you'll be surprised how much life they've got left. Just don't gallop them for hours."

Hank eyed the two prospects and decided Buttercup was at least capable of supporting his weight. Laverne looked as if a trip to the glue factory might be a mercy, but Becky wouldn't hear of such a thing and assured him Laverne was capable of carrying Carly.

He struggled to saddle the two horses, and Carly came bouncing back from the house with a picnic lunch wrapped up in a canvas satchel. She had added a sweater and a down-filled vest to her ensemble and looked like a city slicker ready for a trail ride. Hank dutifully added her picnic to their overstuffed saddlebags.

"Why do we need all this stuff?" he whispered to Becky when she added more gear to Buttercup's load.

"You never know what might happen," Becky murmured back.

"You don't suppose Laverne's going to kick the bucket on this trip?" Hank asked, nervously watching as Carly petted the Appaloosa's spotted nose.

"I was thinking more along the lines of you getting lost," Becky retorted. She jerked her head to indicate Carly. "Help her into the saddle, hero."

"This is so exciting!" Carly cried as Hank boosted her up onto Laverne. She didn't notice as Laverne let out a gusty sigh of resignation. Fortunately Carly also didn't seem to grasp the elderly condition of either one of the horses Becky had selected for them.

Hank took his courage in hand and hauled himself into Buttercup's slippery saddle.

Despite all the years he'd spent in the great outdoors, Hank had never mastered the art of riding and tended to spend most of his horseback time hyperventilating. He was athletic enough in other sports, but the skills required for sitting on a moving horse continued to elude him. Long ago he'd decided it was probably a mental block brought on by some psychological reasoning that only a few decades of psychotherapy could fix.

But instead of seeing a shrink, he just stayed away from horses.

This time that wasn't possible.

Becky gave Carly a few quick instructions about riding Laverne and made Carly practice some turns around the corral. Satisfied after several minutes, Becky nodded and opened the gate. "You're a natural," she called to Carly.

To Hank, Becky whispered, "Nobody could fall off Laverne even if they tried. But Buttercup—well, you'd better be a little careful with her. She has a stubborn streak."

Hank groaned. With trepidation, he urged Buttercup after Laverne as Carly headed out of the ranch gate. He ignored his sister's big grin and concentrated on balancing in the saddle. Silently, Hank prayed he could get through the day without breaking any bones.

Passing through the gate, Buttercup gave an almost frisky swish of her tail as if she were happy to be setting off on an adventure. Hank clutched the saddle horn to keep his balance and cursed under his breath.

Heading away from the ranch, Carly inhaled a deep gulp of South Dakota air. The morning had turned deliciously warm, and the air was so clear it almost hurt to breathe it. From astride her horse, Laverne, Carly could see for miles, and the country was exquisitely beautiful.

"I could get used to this."

"Beg pardon?"

Carly stammered, not realizing she'd spoken aloud and that Hank was just a few paces behind her. "I...I was just thinking, well, as long as a person has to live someplace, it might as well be as pretty as this."

Hank urged his horse forward and angled the animal so that his knee made contact with Carly's in a friendly bump. "I had you pegged for a confirmed city girl."

"Oh, I am. But this is magnificent!"

She spread one arm to indicate the panorama around them. The Black Hills rose ponderously over a seemingly endless green- and wheat-flecked prairie. Stands of aspen trees shivered in the slight breeze, their colors shifting like a shimmering waterfall. The cloudless sky was infinite and a shade of blue Carly had never seen before.

"It's gorgeous," she added with a sigh. "Makes me glad to be alive."

To be honest, Hank's proximity contributed most to Carly's high spirits. It was amazing how much an attractive man on a horse could lift a girl's mood. Glad to have the mouthwatering cowboy all to herself, she sent him a grin. "What should we do first?"

"First?" he asked, raising one bemused brow.

"Well, I'd like to work up an appetite before we have our picnic," she said smoothly. "How exactly do we look for strays?"

He shrugged. "Think like a cow, I guess."

"You mean, try to figure out where they'd be hiding?"

"Yeah, that's it."

"I see. Well, if I were a cow, I'd want to be under those trees over there." She pointed toward a stand of woods at the base of the mountain. "Wouldn't you?"

"It's as good a place to start as any."

"Great. I'll race you!"

Carly booted Laverne just like she'd seen in Western movies and was rewarded by a yelping shout from Hank and a lumbering gallop from her horse. Clinging to the saddle and a handful of mane, Carly whooped with delight. The wind whipped through her hair. The thunder of pounding hooves filled her ears. She could hear Hank's horse breathing down her neck as they tore across a wide field, heading for the trees.

She laughed with delight. It *was* like riding a carousel horse—a smooth rhythm as she sat in the rocking-chairlike saddle.

At last, however, Laverne slowed down and jumped over a trickle of a stream. The landing jolted Carly almost out of her saddle, and she was glad her horse trotted to a halt within a few yards. Breathlessly she clumsily turned Laverne around to find out what had happened to Hank.

Startled, she saw that he'd gotten off his horse and

was hunkered down, studying some marks in the soft earth near the stream.

Carly trotted Laverne over to him to see what he was doing.

"What have you found?"

Hank got up quickly—or was it stiffly?—and used his hat to brush dust from his jeans. "Oh, I was just looking at some tracks, that's all."

Carly hadn't noticed before that his jeans were so filthy. "You didn't fall off your horse just now, did you?"

"Of course not!" He looked offended. "I just—a ranch isn't the cleanest place on earth, that's all. I found some wolf tracks."

"Wolf tracks!" Carly forgot about Hank's jeans. "You're sure?"

Hank pointed to the ground. "See for yourself."

"Those look like dog tracks to me. Maybe Charlie was out here—"

"Charlie doesn't leave the rug in the living room," Hank told her. "No, this is a wolf, I'm sure."

"The one we heard howling last night?"

"Maybe."

"Those are awfully big tracks."

"Which means we probably have an awfully big wolf in the neighborhood."

Carly shivered. "Should we turn back?"

Hank weighed his options. Death at the jaws of a wild beast? Or death by humiliation if he returned to the ranch and had to show Carly what an amateur he really was?

He manufactured a cowboy drawl. "I reckon we'll be safe enough."

"Okay, but let's stick together, all right?"

"Whatever you say."

He climbed back into the saddle, thankful that Carly hadn't seen the tumble he'd taken just moments earlier. His whole body ached despite his precaution of taking two aspirins before leaving the ranch. His good luck had held, too. Finding the wolf tracks when he landed in the dust had been nothing short of miraculous.

"Let's head for those trees," he said as he authoritatively set off in the lead. Buttercup plodded along as quietly as an old donkey who'd never dream of pitching off her rider, but her ears were alert for the next opportunity for mischief. Hank vowed to be more careful of Buttercup's sly ways.

"Look!" Carly cried suddenly. "There's a cow!"

Hank prayed she was seeing things. "Where?"

"There!" She stood in her stirrups and pointed excitedly. "That's a stray, right?"

Sure enough, a white-faced Hereford wandered out from behind the line of trees about two hundred yards away. Hank stifled a groan. He had no desire to start chasing down half-wild cows. "Well, it could be one of the neighbor's herd," he cautioned. "We'll have to check the brand."

"How do we do that? Let's go!"

There was no stopping her. She booted her horse into a lumbering gallop so that Hank had no choice but to follow her again. He clutched his saddle horn for dear life as Buttercup pounded after Carly's horse. The tall grass whipped against Hank's stirrups.

He prayed there weren't any gopher holes for Buttercup to step into.

"Yii—ha!" Carly cried.

The steer looked up from grazing, startled to have his morning snack interrupted. It took one look at Carly and snorted belligerently.

"Carly, wait!"

But she urged Laverne ahead, and the steer suddenly turned and made a surprisingly agile dash into the trees.

"Get your rope!" Carly yelled over her shoulder. "Don't you have to lasso him?"

Actually, Hank had once been pretty good with a rope. When he'd been growing up, practicing with twenty-five feet of hemp had been a hell of a lot easier than helping with any ranch chores. But picking up his rope meant letting go of his stranglehold on the saddle horn.

"Come on!" Carly shouted. "He's getting away!"

You're out of options, pal, Hank thought.

He made a grab for his rope. Buttercup seemed to know what to do, and she dove excitedly into the brush after the Hereford. Hank hung on, struggled with the rope for an instant, then managed to make a loop—all the while plunging deeper and deeper into the thick bushes. Buttercup snorted and leaped a culvert. Hank held back a yelp.

Then, suddenly, there was the steer, and Hank's rope was ready. He threw it instinctively, and a miracle occurred. The steer threw his head directly into the loop. Buttercup jolted to a stop, the steer kept running and the rope played out smoothly.

The steer reached the end of the line, Buttercup braced herself, and suddenly everything was perfect.

Except that Hank had forgotten to wrap his end of the rope around the saddle horn. He went sailing right over Buttercup's head.

Carly shrieked.

Hank landed on the hard ground with a thump. His prey took off like a rocket, and a second later Hank's arm was yanked out of its socket one more time. Suddenly he was being dragged through the brush. His mouth was full of dirt, his belly scraped the rocks and his belt buckle practically made sparks as he flew along the earth.

"Whoa!" he bellowed, his panicked brain temporarily malfunctioning.

Then he slammed into a tree. His momentum whirled him around on his belly, but Hank still couldn't make himself let go of the rope. It tightened around the tree, and he heard a thunderous crash nearby.

"Wonderful!" Carly cried, panting as she leaped down from her horse. "That was perfect!"

"P-perfect?"

"You caught him! He's still on the ground! Is he stunned?" Carly threw herself down beside Hank's prone body. "Should I check the brand? I thought you were supposed to stay on your horse. Wow, this is exciting!"

She kept talking, but she might as well have been speaking Russian. Hank couldn't think. Dizzily he sat up on one elbow. He shook his head to get rid of the stars that swam in his line of vision. He spat the dust from his mouth and squinted at the Hereford that he'd managed to stop purely by accident.

The steer scrambled up and shook himself off. Dust flew from his thick coat. But he stood docilely at the end of the rope, realizing he'd been beaten.

Painfully, Hank got to his feet, too. His ears were ringing. The scratches on his stomach stung. He couldn't catch his breath.

But he pulled himself together with all the concentration of an Oscar-winning actor.

"All in a day's work," he said gruffly, hoping like hell he hadn't broken any ribs.

Starry-eyed, Carly watched as Hank reeled in the rest of his rope and approached the steer.

The animal was breathing hard, but it was unafraid of Hank. Hank risked patting its shoulder. With a jerk of its head, the steer snorted, but didn't try to fight him. Hank ran his hand along the rough fur and looked for a brand.

"Aha," he said, at last spotting a mark on the beast's hip. "See this symbol? That's the Conner brand. This steer isn't ours."

"You'll have to let it go?"

Hank was already removing the rope from the steer's neck. "Yep."

Disappointed, Carly sighed. "Darn. It seems so anticlimactic. The first real cow roping I've ever seen, and you have to let it go."

"That's life out here in the West," Hank said cheerily. *And, thank God, I'm still alive,* he thought.

But Carly looked truly sorry as Hank turned the steer loose. It bolted for cover in the bushes once again. "I guess we'll just have to keep searching," she said on a disappointed sigh. "Oh, no, look!"

Hank wheeled around. Buttercup kicked up her heels and joyously headed back to the ranch at a gallop, clearly delighted to find herself free as a bird.

Hank was willing to bet Buttercup wasn't as happy as he was, however.

But he concocted some fake anger for Carly's benefit. "Damnation!"

"She's going back to the ranch!" Carly cried. "Is she supposed to do that?"

"No," Hank snapped. Then, for the sake of authenticity, he added, "I've been training her lately. I guess all the lessons haven't sunk in yet."

"Training her to do what?"

"Well, you know, ranch stuff."

"Should I go after her?"

To be truthful, Hank was immensely relieved to be rid of the horse. But he had to find a way to hide his relief from Carly. "Uh, no," he said. "You might get hurt chasing around the countryside. Just let her go."

"But what will you do?"

"This isn't the first time I've had to walk."

"I thought cowboys hated to lose their horses."

"Oh, we do," Hank assured her. "But it happens."

He found himself standing very close to Carly, and she was staring up at him with a shine of admiration in her eyes.

They were very pretty eyes, too, he had to admit.

Looking down at her, Hank forgot about his aches and pains. He forgot about acting like an idiot. He began to think like an ordinary, red-blooded American male and decided it would be an easy matter to gather her up in his arms and kiss the stuffing out of Carly then and there. His mouth got very dry.

She had to be thinking about the same idea because her gaze turned shadowy. "I...I guess we could share my horse, couldn't we? Ride double, I mean?"

"Well, we wouldn't want to tire out Laverne."

Carly looked momentarily disappointed. "We wouldn't?"

"I don't mind walking, really."

She frowned a little. "Maybe I'd better walk, too. To avoid getting saddle sore."

"Well, if you think that's best..."

She smiled up at him again. "I think we'd better stick close together. I'd hate to get lost out here."

"Me, too."

"What?"

"I mean, I'd hate for you to get lost," he corrected himself. "Shall we?"

Hank hesitated for only an instant. "That way." He pointed with a great deal more confidence than he was feeling.

They gathered up Laverne's reins and set off walking over the rough terrain, Hank pushing brush out of their way as they progressed through the thicket. Already, he could feel his body tightening up from the two falls he'd taken so far. He forced himself not to limp, but the muscles in his back had begun to protest.

With your luck, you'll end up in traction before this day is over, he told himself.

Carly didn't seem to notice any signs of his physical weaknesses. She blathered on about how exciting and dramatic her first roundup was, how she'd never seen anything as breathtaking as Hank riding into the brush with his rope around the cow's neck.

"Steer," Hank corrected her.

"Oh, really? I suppose you think I'm a complete greenhorn."

"Everybody's a greenhorn at the beginning."

"Except you," she pointed out. "You've lived and breathed this life from the cradle, haven't you?"

With time out for the real world, he wanted to say. But he allowed Carly to rhapsodize without interrupting after that. He decided he rather liked listening to her voice. It kept his mind off his injuries, at least.

They found their way out of the tangled brush and ended up on a trail Hank didn't recognize at first.

"Where are we?" Carly asked, holding up one hand to shield her eyes from the sun. "Is the ranch very far?"

"This way, I think."

"You think?"

"The land is constantly changing," he told her. "Grass grows, streams change course, trees fall."

"Oh, yes, of course." She nodded sagely. "This isn't exactly a suburban backyard, is it? There must be thousands of acres to memorize."

"You learn to look for landmarks, that's all."

She pointed. "Like that stream down there?"

"Exactly. Let's go." Hank led the way, with Carly and Laverne following behind.

They scrambled down a hillside and ended up by a stream that Hank felt pretty certain they had not crossed earlier. But Laverne was happy to slurp up water and almost pulled Carly into the stream as she waded knee-deep for a drink. Hank caught Carly around the waist just in time to save her from falling in.

"Oh, thanks," Carly gasped, leaning back against him as he gripped her body.

"Don't fall," he cautioned, unwilling to let her go just yet. "Hand me the reins."

Obediently Carly shifted Laverne's reins to his hand, and Laverne chose that moment to plunge deeper into the stream. Yanked off balance, Hank teetered on a stone. He felt it tilt under his weight.

Carly felt it, too, and yelped. She twisted in his embrace and seized Hank in a bear hug. "Hang on!"

He almost went into the stream. One boot slid off the slippery stone, sending him downward, but Hank managed to land his butt on the rocks and avoid getting soaked. Then Carly crashed down beside him and slithered out of control toward the water. Hank grabbed her arm, braced himself on a stone, and they both stopped just inches from the stream.

"Wow," Carly panted, laughing. "This is a real adventure, isn't it?"

Hank held back a few choice curses and hauled Carly back up to safety. They collapsed on the bank together in a tangle of arms and legs.

Her laughter faded. Abruptly Hank found himself sitting with his nose barely six inches from Carly's and her startled gaze wide on his.

Hank's mental circuits once again went on the fritz. Carly's full mouth suddenly looked quite delectable, and Hank wondered if those lips tasted as delicious as they looked. For a painful heartbeat, he thought about kissing her to find out.

The moment lengthened, and Carly didn't move. She felt pliant in his grasp and didn't draw back.

Kiss her, you idiot, screamed his inner voice.

But a sudden snort brought them both back to reality. In unison, they looked toward the source of the snort.

Laverne stood in the water and looked placidly at them as if enjoying a mildly entertaining vaudeville show. Water dripped from her mouth, and her reins trailed downstream.

"Oh, dear," Carly moaned. "I shouldn't have let her loose. She'll run away, won't she? And take our lunch!"

Losing the horse didn't bother Hank. But the idea of losing his lunch was a different proposition altogether. Suddenly he was famished.

"C'mere, Laverne," Hank coaxed, getting up on one knee. "There's a good girl."

"Here, Laverne," Carly cooed.

Hank yanked a handful of succulent grass from the ground and held it out temptingly to the horse. "See, Laverne? A nice snack. Come and get it."

Laverne looked at the two of them down her long nose as if to say, "I'm not as stupid as you think I am."

"Laverne!" Carly commanded, sounding like a dog trainer. "Come!"

But Laverne shook her head and took a giant step backward in the water.

"You stay here," Hank commanded Carly as he got to his feet.

"What are you doing?"

"I've got to catch her. She's got our lunch."

"Let me help."

"Any suggestions?"

Carly thought the situation over for two seconds, then said, "I can climb over those rocks and circle around behind her. We'll have her trapped."

"Not a bad idea."

"I'll go over this way." Carly pointed downstream.

Hank nodded. "Just don't scare her."

"Right."

Unsteadily Hank inched his way down to the stream again and stepped cautiously onto a large flat stone. He hopped none too gracefully to another stone, conscious that Laverne never took her suspicious brown eyes off him. He made a flying leap for the other bank. He landed with a squish in some mud, pirouetted and made a grab for Laverne's reins.

At that moment, Carly gave a bloodcurdling scream.

Four

Laverne gave a terrified squeal and nearly knocked Hank over as she thrashed out of the water. Luckily, Hank got a grip on one rein and managed to prevent the horse from galloping back to the ranch with her stirrups flying. Then he spun around to face whatever danger Carly confronted.

But she was splashing clumsily through the icy stream toward him, blathering in terror. "It's dead, it's dead, it's dead!"

"What? What's dead?"

"It—it—it!" She threw herself into his arms and nearly knocked him off his feet again.

Hank spun her around and plunked her on the bank. "Easy, easy. What did you see?"

She pointed a trembling forefinger toward the rocks across the stream. "I...it...I think—"

Putting his hands on her shoulders, Hank squeezed her into calm. "Take a deep breath. Whatever it is, if it's dead, it can't hurt you."

Carly nodded in panicky jerks. "Right. I know that. I know that."

"Want me to go look?"

She reversed her nods into sideways shakes of her head, her hair spraying water. "No. No, it's a wolf. At least, I think so."

"A dead wolf?"

She shuddered and managed another nod. "It must have been shot or something. It's right over there—"

"Okay, I'm going to check. Can you hold Laverne?"

"I think so." She accepted the reins, but her hands were shaking.

Hank steeled himself for the worst and climbed back across the stream to locate the animal that had frightened Carly. Among some tumbled rocks, he did find the carcass of a wolf. The gray fur was unmistakable. The animal lay half in the water, half on the bank as if it had come to drink and simply fallen in exhaustion. But when Hank put on one of his gloves and pulled the wolf the rest of the way out of the water, he saw differently.

He hunkered down, half to settle his roiling stomach. Bullet wounds had ravaged the magnificent animal.

The wolf hadn't been dead long enough to start decomposing, he noted, so it must have been shot recently.

From across the stream, Carly called timidly, "Is it really dead?"

Hank stood up. "I'm afraid so. You were right. Someone's shot it."

"Is that legal?"

Hank wasn't sure what laws existed in the state anymore, so he decided not to answer. He made his way back across the rocks to Carly and Laverne. "We'll have to see that it gets buried. I'll come back later with a shovel."

Carly shivered. "How awful."

Putting his arm across her shoulders, Hank said, "We can't do anything to help it now."

"Do you think it was the wolf we heard last night?"

"Possibly," Hank murmured. Then, seeing that Carly was about to cry, he said, "Maybe not. Look, we'd better get back to the ranch. You're soaked to the skin."

Carly finally noticed that she had managed to get completely wet when she ran through the stream. She stepped shakily out of his embrace and swiped her hair from her eyes. "You're right. Sorry. Ugh, even my sneakers."

She took a couple of steps backward, shoes squishing. "Boy, I've really made a mess of things, haven't I? I'm not usually skittish, but—"

She interrupted herself to scream again.

This time, Hank almost screamed, too. From beneath her sneaker jumped a small, furry animal. It yipped and latched its teeth onto Carly's jeans. She yelped and tried to shake free of the attacking beast. With a sudden, squealing cry, it let go and plunked back to earth.

"What the hell?"

"Oh, my goodness!" Carly cried. "It's a puppy!"

"It's a *wolf!*"

"Oh, what a darling!"

"For godsake, don't pick it up!"

But Carly wasn't listening. Suddenly turning into a saint of the Humane Society, she bent down and scooped up the whimpering beast. It fought against her grasp. "Oh," she cooed despite the animal's obvious dislike for humans. "Isn't she wonderful?"

"It's a wild animal," Hank snapped. "It's not a pet. Put it down!"

Carly buried her nose in the pup's fur and didn't appear to notice that it began snapping at her hair. "Oh, you poor, poor sweetheart!"

"Watch out. It might eat your arm."

"Oh, she can't hurt a fly. Look at her sweet face!"

Sweet was hardly the word Hank was thinking of. "Put it down before it starts thinking you're friendly."

"I *am* friendly." Carly held the pup away from herself and looked into its eyes with a sappy smile on her mouth. The pup was suddenly entranced by Carly's face. "What will you do without your mama? We can't possibly leave you here alone, can we?"

"Of course we can," Hank said ominously. "What are you thinking, Carly?"

"That she'll die out here alone. If she doesn't starve, some idiot will shoot her."

"Wait a second. You've got to be sensible about this!"

She looked up at Hank and tucked the squirming

pup under her arm like a football. "You're not going to suggest we abandon this poor baby?"

"I'm not suggesting—I'm telling you straight out! We can't take that animal home like it was a cocker spaniel from the nearest pet shop!"

"She's too young to survive on her own."

"It's not an infant," Hank pointed out. "It's young, but it's old enough to kill a few field mice to eat. Look at that thing! It's actually chewing you!"

Indeed, the pup was gnawing on Carly's wristwatch. She laughingly pushed its snout away. "Teething, that's all it is."

"Those are some teeth," Hank observed darkly.

"I'm taking her back to the ranch," Carly said, and the look in her eye indicated there would be no argument.

Laverne, being a sensible, domesticated animal, refused to get close to the pup. She stretched out her rein as far as she could to get away from the wolf, snorting and shying and otherwise making her message very clear. *Either the pup goes,* she seemed to say, *or I do.*

To Carly, Hank said, "How do you propose to do it? Laverne won't let you in the saddle while you're holding that thing. And you're soaking wet. You'll probably catch pneumonia before we get home."

"Then we'll have to build a fire and dry out, I guess."

"That will take hours!"

Carly glared at him. "I'm not leaving this baby!"

Hank glared back at her. For a long moment he considered his options. Climbing aboard Laverne and heading back to the ranch for help seemed like a logical choice, but leaving a woman out in the wilderness was hardly the gentlemanly thing to do. Besides, Hank wasn't absolutely sure he would be able to find her again if he left the area. As he glared at Carly, her teeth began to chatter with cold.

He sighed. "All right. I'll build a fire."

Carly smiled through the chattering. "Thank you. What can I do to help?"

Hank left her sitting on a fallen log, cuddling the pup in her arms and talking baby talk to it. As he tied up Laverne and set about gathering kindling and a couple of chunks of firewood, he could hear Carly laughing softly at her newfound friend.

Well, he thought, *at least we're out of Becky's way today.*

With that thought to comfort him, it didn't take long to locate enough dried sticks and bits of wood to make a decent fire. In time, Hank cleared a spot and carefully laid the wood in a Boy Scout-approved pattern. All his time hiking and climbing in rough country had taught him the value of a well-laid fire.

Carly produced a cigarette lighter from her pocket to start the blaze, and soon they were watching smoke rise from the snapping flames.

But the fire wasn't going to be enough, he saw. Carly was soaked and still shivering.

"You'd better take off some of those wet clothes," Hank observed. "They'll dry faster that way."

"You're right," she said, looking miserable. "Will you hold her for me?"

Hank didn't have much choice. Carly thrust the pup at him, and he automatically accepted the bristling bundle. Awkwardly, however, he held the pup's squirming body away from himself and hoped it wouldn't bite his thumb off. The wolf's beady gaze had latched onto the thumb like a guided missile homing in on a target.

"She can't hurt you," Carly said, not trying very hard to hide her grin as she unzipped her down-filled vest.

"Have you explained that to her?" Hank asked.

Carly couldn't answer, since she was in the act of pulling her wet cable-knit sweater over her head. As the sopping sweater came off, Hank couldn't help noticing how snugly her remaining wet shirt clung to her figure. She was literally soaked to the skin, but somehow she managed to look very attractive at the same time.

She draped the wet sweater over the spare firewood and regarded her shirt. "Boy, I really did a number on myself, didn't I?"

"You're awfully wet."

"Not to mention uncomfortable."

"At the risk of sounding like a desperate man at last call, let me say that you should probably take all those wet things off."

She bit her lower lip, considering the problem for a moment, then lifted her bemused gaze to his. "We can be adult about this, can't we?"

"I haven't leered at a half-dressed woman in at least a decade."

"For some reason, I doubt that."

"Well, I haven't leered in several months, at least."

"That sounds more realistic." She reached for the

buttons on her shirt. "Here goes, anyway. I'm sure my clothes will dry faster if I take them off."

"Right." Despite his good intentions, Hank was quite unable to tear his eyes from the sight she made standing there with the sunlight rendering the wet shirt nearly invisible.

His mind whirled and blocked out all other thoughts when Carly's shirt came off. Her bra was pale pink satin and looked as expensive as it did sexy. The garment perfectly shaped her breasts and covered them with delicate lace that made Hank's mouth go dry.

Clearly, she had taken time to select her underclothes with care, and Hank's imagination began conjuring up scenes of Carly shopping for lingerie. Did she try on everything, he wondered, in dressing rooms with lots of mirrors?

When she sat down and took off her boots and socks, he discreetly turned his back and congratulated himself on being a gentleman after all.

"I can't very well take off my jeans," Carly said from behind him. "I'm not that brave."

"Don't let me stop you."

"I'm just a little damp."

Hank risked a peek and noticed that her jeans were every bit as soaked as the rest of her clothing. But he refrained from pointing out the obvious. He handed her the pup. "I'll check Laverne's saddlebag. There's bound to be something you can wrap up in."

"That would be great. Thanks."

He almost fell over the log on his way to look into the saddlebag. Laverne turned her head and glowered witheringly at him, however, which shamed Hank into pulling himself together. There was no sense acting like a hormone-incensed schoolboy. Within moments, he had rummaged through some of the gear Becky had packed and found two red plaid blankets. He carried them back for Carly to use.

She had put the pup down on the ground, and it was determinedly pouncing on one of Carly's wet socks. Carly had picked up the other end of the sock and they played tug-of-war. She looked up at his return. "Any luck?"

"More than I expected. There are *two* blankets and a tent, too, if you'd like total privacy."

"Do you know how to put a tent together?"

"Of course." Unfolding the first blanket for her, he said, "Your wish is my command."

"To be honest, I'd rather have some lunch. I'm really starving. I packed a picnic, you know. I hope it wasn't on the other horse."

"I'll check Laverne's other bag."

He located the picnic, which consisted of wrapped sandwiches, four bottles of beer and a thermos of something hot. It only took a couple of minutes to unsaddle Laverne and leave her tied close enough to a thatch of grass to keep her happy for an hour or two.

Meanwhile Carly had stretched the first blanket out on the ground, and she reclined on it, loosely wrapping the second one around her shoulders. It was determined to slip off as she continued playing with the pup. With the sunlight spilling over the red blanket, her body looked slim and white. Hank hesitated, standing over her.

"Come on, sit down," she said, moving aside to

make room for him beside her in the glow of the fire. "Down here out of the breeze, it's really quite warm. Don't you think so?"

The blanket was relatively comfortable, Hank decided, and sitting next to Carly was exactly the way he'd prefer to spend the afternoon. He unwrapped their lunch and tried to keep his gaze from devouring *her* instead of the food. He was suddenly quite hungry.

"I hope you don't mind my choice for lunch," Carly said. "I made sandwiches from what I could find in the kitchen. There were olives in the fridge. Do you suppose Becky was saving them for a special occasion? I love olives. And there's hot coffee, too."

"You are a saint," Hank said, unwrapping the olives from plastic wrap and offering some to her. The ripe black olives had come to the ranch in Hank's suitcase from his favorite deli in Seattle, and he couldn't imagine a more special occasion to celebrate their deliciousness. He helped himself when Carly began popping her share into her mouth one by one. She moaned with happiness as the flavor exploded in her mouth, and he couldn't help smiling at her pleasure. He asked, "Beer or coffee with this feast?"

She shared his smile, still savoring the olives. "I rarely drink beer, but somehow it's right here. Let's save the coffee for later, shall we?"

The beer wasn't quite cold, but the sandwiches were perfect—slices of Becky's own smoked turkey on whole wheat bread with lettuce, mayo and a hint of dill. Hank's estimation of Carly's character rose even higher. A woman who knew how to make a good sandwich was worth ten who could prepare an elaborate dinner party.

Carly fed a bite to the pup, and it immediately began nosing around for more food. It ate a whole sandwich with quick dispatch, then plunked down on the blanket and licked its chops as if complimenting the chef. A moment later it flopped down and prepared to go to sleep.

Obviously Hank soon felt the same way—sated and appreciative. He took off his hat and lounged back on one elbow to finish his beer and enjoy the sunshine and radiating heat of the fire.

Carly ruffled the wolf's fur, but found herself staring at Hank instead. He looked at ease and contented, stretched out on the blanket with the beer bottle cradled against his chest. The picture of a sexy man at rest.

At last she ventured to say, "This would be the ideal moment to take those preliminary photographs.

He opened one eye to look at her. "Sorry to disappoint you, but your cameras were in Buttercup's saddlebags. They're probably back at the ranch by now."

She sighed. "Darn. You look perfect right now."

He snorted a laugh and closed his eyes again. "I can't figure out why you'd pick me of all people for this calendar thing."

"Because you're—well, you're a normal guy who happens to be very appealing to women. You're not plastic or—well, you don't look as if you spend all your spare time at the gym admiring your pecs in the mirror. You're just sexier than most."

"I am, huh? You're the first to notice."

Carly shook her head. "I'm sure I'm not the first."

"Okay, maybe not. But I'm not exactly fighting off the opposite sex all the time."

"Because you live out here in the middle of nowhere," Carly guessed.

"That's not it."

"You don't think you're an attractive man?"

He grinned. "Let's just say I'm hard to get along with."

Carly found herself intrigued. She was glad he had his eyes closed against the sunlight, because she wanted to absorb everything about him just then. "Why are you hard to get along with?"

He shrugged and tried to think of a way to explain himself without going into detail about his double life—that of a responsible journalist with deadlines to keep and his other half—the outdoorsman who enjoyed his free time. Most women had a hard time keeping his two halves straight.

One former girlfriend had said succinctly, "You only want a part-time lover, Henry."

She'd been right, he thought. Any woman who wanted to be with Henry Fowler had to have a life of her own. She couldn't depend upon him to provide constant attention and entertainment. He was too busy.

Carefully he said, "I like having things my own way. And I'm getting too old to be flexible."

"You're spoiled."

He laughed. "Yeah, that's probably it."

"That's why you're not married?"

"I've come close," he said. "A couple of times. But..."

"What happened?"

"Oh, nothing unusual. Everybody has different expectations. I guess my former girlfriends have been disappointed when I didn't measure up."

"In bed, you mean?"

"No, no. Sex is always good," he said with another grin. He was surprised at Carly's line of questioning, but plunged ahead with his answer. "Sometimes it's fabulous. No, it's the emotional stuff that's complicated. I've been grown-up a long time, and I'm not looking for a mother. I enjoy being with women who are independent and don't fuss over me all the—" He caught himself and opened his eyes. "Why am I talking about myself again?"

"Because I'm interested. Let's get back to the fabulous part again."

With a laugh he asked, "Are you thinking about fabulous sex every time you make a calendar?"

"I try to," Carly said honestly. "It's harder than you imagine. I have to think about what *other* women want when I plan a calendar. Hiring the models, arranging the shots, setting up—it makes me weary sometimes. Bringing all those female fantasies to life is hard work."

By that, his attention was aroused completely. "What kinds of female fantasies? You mean firefighters wielding their big axes and wearing no shirts?"

"Sure," she said on a laugh. "And our police officer calendar sold well."

"Did they carry big nightsticks and take off their shirts?"

"You bet."

"What about the cowboy calendar? I'm supposed to carry a big gun and take off my shirt, huh?"

"It's not just a matter of props and missing clothing," Carly corrected. "There has to be a certain look in a man's eye."

"What does a cop's eye look like?"

"Tough. Dangerous. Like he's thinking about arresting someone."

"And a firefighter?"

"Noble. He's about to run out and rescue little children from burning buildings, you know. But he also has to look a little dangerous, too."

"Dangerous seems to be a theme. And what kind of look is the cowboy supposed to have in his eye?"

"I don't know exactly. But you have it right now. What are you thinking about?"

Hank never hesitated. "I'm thinking I've never seen a woman look so sexy in her underwear."

Carly laughed and felt herself turn hot. "What else are you thinking?"

"That I'd like to be kissing her right now," he replied steadily.

Carly took a deep breath and looked deeply into his glowing blue gaze. She couldn't hold back an answering smile and thought that sometimes a girl just had to take matters into her own hands. Or lips.

She leaned toward Hank, then hesitated. For an instant she wondered what his kiss might taste like, but then suddenly she knew. He met her halfway. He was warm and sweet and delicious, and Carly wanted the moment to last at least an hour.

But she pulled back and blinked into his eyes, wondering if she was crazy or just temporarily insane. Carly Cortazzo didn't do this sort of thing—take off her clothes and eat a picnic in her underwear as calmly as you please, then start kissing a man she'd known only a day.

"I...I'm sorry," she murmured, staring into his eyes with something like terror welling up inside herself. "I'm not usually like this."

"Like what?"

"Reckless and—well, impatient."

Hank didn't seem to have any such reservations. In another moment, he wound his hand around the nape of her neck and sank his fingers into her hair as if enjoying its silky texture. Pulling gently, he drew Carly's mouth against his own once again. The contact was firmer this time, more intense. He made a noise in the back of his throat—not a groan exactly, but a sound of pleasure. It made Carly melt inside, and her lips turned pliant against his.

As a rush of erotic sensations grew inside her, Carly wrapped one slim arm around his neck and found herself pressing up against the soft flannel of his shirt. She could feel his heart beating against hers. His breath was deep and even—counterpointing her own increasingly breathless state. Then Hank swiped his tongue along her lower lip in a wonderfully casual exploration that caused Carly to shudder with anticipation.

A heartbeat later he was kissing her throat, her neck, her bare shoulder. Somehow her bra strap was sliding off into oblivion, and Carly found herself holding on to Hank just to stay on earth.

"Oh, boy," she began to chant mindlessly. "Oh, boy, oh, boy..."

"Too fast," Hank responded hoarsely, lips against her bare skin. "I know it's too fast. We'd better stop."

"We'd better," Carly agreed, her head tilted up to the sky and her mind swimming in the clouds. "But don't. Don't stop. Not yet."

"You're delicious," he murmured. "I love your skin. So soft."

Beneath the flannel of his shirt, Carly could feel the contour of Hank's shoulders, his strong arms, his chest. The suggestion of taut, smooth muscles tempted her fingertips. His shirt buttons came unfastened slowly, and Hank made no move to stop her progress.

His thumb swiped deliberately across her breast instead, and Carly couldn't hold back a gasp. "This is crazy. I don't *do* this kind of thing!"

"Not ever?"

"Well, I mean—oh, that's so good—I'm not a teenager anymore. I don't go jumping into bed with men at the drop of—oh, Hank."

"I don't jump, either," he murmured, finding another spot to nibble behind her ear. "Not like this. I'm usually a cautious person."

"Me, too. I don't—don't even *know* you, but—"

"Look, I know this is awkward, but I'm healthy." Hank pulled back and met Carly's gaze squarely. "I mean, I'm okay, Carly. I get checkups every year and all the tests are routine nowadays."

"I hate talking about this. You're the first man I've ever known to bring it up on his own."

"I guess I've learned to overcome the embarrassment."

"I'm impressed. And glad. I'm careful, too." She smiled, suddenly glad she had found a man she could actually say these things to without humiliation.

Laying her cards on the table with Hank felt right. Without taking her eyes from his, Carly managed to slip his shirt off at last. Next she began to roll up the hem of the T-shirt he wore underneath. With one hand, she found the bare skin of his chest and slid her fingers through the crisp hair. "My doctor is very thorough, but I don't really do things that could get me into trouble in the first place."

"Me, neither."

"But you're—this is different for me. Are we being stupid?"

"Maybe." He used one finger to slide her other bra strap out of the way.

"Should we stop?"

"Maybe," he said again, but pressed another kiss on her shoulder.

"I—I don't really want to."

By himself, Hank finished the job of peeling off his T-shirt. Their skin felt electric as they rubbed together in the cool air.

"Thing is," he said roughly, "I didn't exactly come prepared. I mean, I didn't expect to end up like this with you and I didn't bring anything—"

"Damn," said Carly, both hands smoothing along his bare chest. "Me, neither."

"We should wait."

"But—"

"Yes?"

"I can't wait."

Hank rolled and pinned Carly gently to the blanket, managing to unfasten her bra with one hand. "I guess," he whispered against her mouth, "we'll have to get creative."

"Oh," Carly whispered, already drowning in exquisite sensations. "Sounds fabulous."

Five

Hours later—or perhaps it was days for all Hank could remember—the fire in his belly burned hotter than ever before, while the fire he'd built with a few pieces of wood had burned down to nothing but smoldering ashes.

With Carly's slim legs entwined with his and her soft curves snuggled up against his harder ones, Hank tried to remember if he'd ever gotten to know a woman's body more intimately than hers without actually climaxing together.

They'd spent the day necking like excited teenagers, then delved into more adult pleasures. Only the strongest part of his character had prevented Hank from tossing caution to the wind and making fierce love with her.

Carly was...erotic, he mused. He hadn't expected

the abandon she'd shared with him. Every inch of her skin had been responsive to his caresses. Every secret place had enticed his touch. He had tasted every inch of her. Remembering the cries that he'd wrenched from Carly just by teasing her with hands and lips, Hank smothered a smile. She was so responsive—quick to arouse and eager to reciprocate.

She'd known her own pleasure, too, while managing to torment Hank to the brink of ecstasy and back again.

He flushed hot at the memory of what she'd done to him during the course of their endless afternoon. She had imagination and no misgivings.

Yet he hadn't given in to the instinct that would make her his completely. Not quite.

Her sweet-smelling hair tickled his nose, and he blew a long breath down the warm column of her throat. He stroked his fingertips down the curve of her hip and thought about how easy it would be to coax her thighs apart and press her down into the blanket to seek the heat at the center of her body.

He felt himself react to the idea, growing tight with desire once again. She was a sexy lady, all right. But there was something more about Carly that appealed to Hank. Her easy laugh was contagious. The sparkle in her eyes made him smile. Her willingness to trust him, to allow Hank to touch her in ways he hadn't really thought of until he'd found himself naked with her—he'd been delighted by that. She trusted him.

But he was lying to her.

If she'd been awake just then, Hank might have spilled the beans about himself. He wasn't the cowboy she thought he was. He was just plain old Henry—a guy from Seattle who took pleasure in many things, but not horses or cattle or whatever romantic notions she imagined in him.

What would she do if he told her the truth?

Probably murder you, he thought suddenly. A wry grin twisted his mouth.

Oh, Carly was a handful, all right. He had a feeling her many passions could include towering rage if she learned she was being duped.

In his arms Carly sighed again and turned a little so that Hank's palm ended up cupping her breast. She smiled and blinked sleepily awake. Her face was still flushed with pleasure, her eyes smoky when they found him half smiling down at her. "Did I fall asleep?"

"It was exhaustion, I think."

"You feel anything but exhausted." Her hand brushed between them and encountered his arousal. She caressed him lightly, looking up into his eyes with a seductive expression growing in her own.

"Are we starting all over again?" Hank asked, tightening in her grasp.

"And again and again."

She began to slide down his body, obviously ready to take him into her mouth again. With more willpower that he knew he had, Hank stopped Carly. Gently he drew her up until their noses were touching. Her breasts were snug against his chest, the nipples boring hot spots into his skin. The sensation made him crazy. But he managed to say quite calmly, "Carly, there's something we should discuss."

"I know, I know." She played her nose around

his. "I have just what we need back at the ranch in my luggage."

"What do you mean?"

"My diaphragm, for one thing. And at least one condom, if we're lucky."

"That's not what I—"

She reached down and stroked him intimately, causing Hank to catch his breath and forget everything but her fingertips. Huskily she said, "I want everything this time."

"Yes," he said, unable to think about anything but the heavenly way she was touching him. "Yes, that's what I want, too."

She sat up, straddling Hank's hips and letting the fading sunlight pour down over her breasts and belly. She continued to caress him, making Hank go dizzy with desire. He closed his eyes and could hardly hear her words when she said, "We'll have to go back to civilization first, I'm afraid."

"Okay, let's go."

"Right now?"

He was drowning in erotic sensations. "Well, not this minute, perhaps."

"Becky will be disappointed we didn't find the stray cattle."

"There's always tomorrow."

Carly sighed and snuggled down on top of him again. "That's one of the things I like about you men of the West."

Hank opened his eyes at that. "What?"

"You haven't let the real world make you nuts."

"I haven't?"

"You're spontaneous. I really like that about you,

Hank. You're natural. Out here in the wild, open spaces with you—I'm a different woman.''

''Uh, different from what?''

''The way I am in L.A. You don't know how important that is to me right now. My responsibilities don't feel so boring. The same old job isn't the focus of every waking moment. Here I can be free, just like you.''

''Well, I'm not completely free.''

''You know what I mean.''

Holding her, Hank considered the situation. If he hadn't been in such a vulnerable position, he might have confessed everything to Carly just then. But he felt sure she was going to be angry.

And maybe disappointed.

Carefully he asked, ''It sounds as if you're under a lot of pressure in L.A.''

''Yes, but pressure doesn't bother me. I love working. I need deadlines and getting out to meet people. I just—well, lately I feel as if I'm not being creative anymore. I need a new outlet, I guess. I'm ready for a change.''

''What kind of change?''

''I don't know yet. Some business venture, I suppose.'' She wisped one long finger along the line of his mustache. ''But don't worry about me. When I think of the right thing, I'll go after it. I don't wait around for opportunities to fall into my lap. I make my own.''

''You're a tough cookie.''

''Not really. I just know what makes me happy. I have to keep myself challenged.'' She smiled. ''That way, my free time is even more enjoyable.''

She leaned down and followed the path of her finger with her mouth, teasing another kiss out of Hank.

She was many things, he thought—career-minded and busy, openhearted and sexy. And always truthful. She hadn't kept any secrets about her life or what she expected from him or Becky with the calendar contest.

No, Carly was an open book.

With more than a twinge of guilt, Hank broke the kiss gently. "Let's get dressed now, okay?"

"If you insist."

"We can be home before nightfall if we hurry."

She blinked up at the sky in surprise. "I didn't realize it was getting so late."

The thought of getting caught outdoors after dark seemed to frighten her. She sat up in a hurry and reached for her jeans—long ago discarded. Fortunately they had been thrown near the fire and seemed mostly dry by now.

Hank sat up, too. "The sun sets pretty quickly out here."

"It does? Did we bring a flashlight? I'm not crazy about darkness, you see, and—oh, Lord!" Her face was the picture of horror. "Where's the pup? Oh, heavens—"

To Hank's dismay, the pup had not wandered off into the wilderness again. Instead, the beast appeared to have slept the whole afternoon. At Carly's exclamation, it scrambled to its feet and gave a huge yawn that displayed a formidable set of sharp puppy teeth.

"Ohh, there you are, Baby."

"Baby, huh?"

Carly tried to catch the pup, but it evaded her warily. She didn't seem daunted, though, and crouched down to coax it closer. "Every living creature needs a name."

"I think Mother Nature might disagree, but Baby it is. Be careful."

Carly almost grabbed the pup, but it veered away and wandered down to the stream for a drink of water. Carly sighed. "Oh, dear."

"Get dressed," Hank suggested, "and we'll try to catch it together."

With any luck, he thought, *it will run away while we're not looking.*

Hank watched Carly dress, sorry to see her naked curves disappear into her clothing once again. He dressed, also, and was glad to find that his socks had dried during the afternoon. His jeans were only slightly damp around the ankles.

When he got to his feet, Hank stretched languidly and looked around for Laverne.

His heart lurched painfully.

"Uh-oh."

Carly looked up from lacing her sneakers. "What's wrong?"

Laverne was not in sight.

Hank squelched the urge to curse his luck and managed to say calmly, "I think we've got a problem."

Carly suppressed screams of terror when she realized they were stranded in the middle of nowhere without a horse—probably for the rest of the night.

"Take it easy." Hank tried to soothe her as he

climbed onto a rock to look around. "Maybe Laverne just wandered off a little."

"I thought horses always returned to their stables."

"Well, usually, yes, but maybe—"

"Why didn't you tie her up?"

"I *did* tie her up. She must have slipped the knot."

"How are we going to survive?" Carly cried, thoroughly panicked.

"It's not a question of survival—just comfort, I'm afraid."

"But—"

"It won't be bad." Hank climbed down from the rock and put a comforting arm across her shoulders. "Look—I took the saddle off her. We have the tent, see?"

"A tent?" Carly tried to control the note of hysteria that threatened to crack her voice. "That's going to keep us safe from wild animals?"

Hank had both arms around her by then. His voice was calm and steadying. "The only wild animals around are your little furry friend and a few field mice, I'm sure. Unless you count me."

Carly let him kiss her neck again, but she couldn't enjoy his attentions. "What about wolves? There must be more of them around."

Hank's lips nibbled her earlobe. "We'll keep a big fire going."

"Oh, my God," Carly moaned, unable to take pleasure in his attentions.

"Think of this as a romantic camping trip."

"The closest I've ever come to camping," she said, attempting to extricate herself gently, "was spending an evening in my car waiting for the auto club to come change a flat tire!''

"How long did you wait?"

"Forty minutes at least!"

"Well, this is going to be a little different." Hank glanced around them to take stock of the situation. "Why don't you scout around for some more firewood while I set up the tent. Then we'll have some of that coffee from the thermos, all right?"

Carly caught his sleeve just as Hank turned purposefully away. "Are we going to starve?"

Hank grinned down at her. "We have at least one sandwich left, right? If we don't give the whole thing to Baby, we'll be fine."

"Hank, I...I'm nervous."

He leaned down and gave her a lingering kiss on the mouth, which should have dissolved all her fears. But at the precise moment when Hank pulled away, a roll of thunder rumbled across the sky overhead. When he looked up at the stormy clouds that had begun to push across from the horizon, Hank couldn't hide his expression of dismay. His reaction did not inspire Carly's confidence.

"Oh, dear," she moaned.

She stumbled into the brush to look for firewood and immediately stepped on a small snake. Things got steadily worse after that.

Turning to run away with a yelp, Carly tripped over a fallen branch and nearly sprawled into a coil of rusted barbed wire. She tore her jeans open at the knee in avoiding a fall. More disasters followed, and in the space of five minutes Carly decided she didn't like South Dakota at all.

She stepped in a squishy puddle of mud and ruined a perfectly good sneaker. Another slip from a rock put grass stains on the rump of her jeans. She unraveled a large portion of one sweater sleeve by catching it on a low-hanging twig. Choking back tears, she returned to their campsite with one stick that was only as big around as her arm.

Hank took a look at the stick, and said, "I don't think that's enough firewood to last the night."

"We're not going to need much firewood," Carly corrected, her heart pounding. "Because it's going to rain any minute. Do you need help with the tent?"

Hank had unpacked a bundle of thin metal rods and some flimsy yellow fabric that hardly looked substantial enough to shelter a rabbit from a spring breeze. He was busily fitting the metal rods together. "No, I'll have this up in a jiffy. Why don't you look for Baby?"

Carly didn't want to explain that she was afraid to venture more than shouting distance from Hank. "I...I think she's wandered off."

"Oh. She'll be back, I'm sure. At least I hope so."

"What?"

Hank hastily changed the subject. "Why don't you pick out a good place for the tent?"

That job sounded like something she could handle. Carly's confidence was at a low ebb, however, and she asked in a small voice, "What kind of place?"

"A dry and flat spot."

Carly looked around and decided the most picturesque location would be the little grassy area beside the creek, just a few yards from their original fire.

To make room for the tent, she picked up a couple of small rocks and threw them into the rushing water.

Hank took a few more minutes to get the tent assembled, and it looked a little crooked when he finally staked it down on the spot Carly showed him. But Carly was glad for the shelter two minutes later when the clouds burst open and dumped a torrential downpour upon them.

She scrambled into the tent to stay dry while Hank collected the rest of their gear and handed it to her. When he hauled Laverne's saddle through the tent flap, however, Carly protested.

"There's hardly room for the two of us let alone that monster!"

"We can't let it get soaked. Becky will kill me."

Over the rush of rain, Carly wasn't sure she'd heard correctly. "What?"

"I mean," he shouted, "it's important to take care of expensive equipment like this."

Carly squished herself into the back of the little tent to make room for Hank and his infernal saddle. The space was very crowded once everything was safely out of the rain, but she bit down on her complaints.

"There," said Hank after he'd zippered them into the tent. "Isn't this cozy?"

"Sure," Carly replied, mustering some enthusiasm. "When can we order from room service?"

"Ouch!" He shifted away from the saddle horn that had poked him in the thigh. "Okay, this isn't exactly the Paris Ritz, but—"

"Don't mention the Ritz right now, okay? I might start crying."

Although he knew Carly was joking, Hank wouldn't mind doing a little crying himself. Despite all the time he'd spent in the great outdoors, there was nothing he'd hated more than camping. And after spending the afternoon on the ground, his whole body was starting to stiffen. He could definitely feel the bruises caused by his assorted injuries that morning. At thirty-seven, he was getting far too old to fall off horses. He shook the rain out of his hair.

What I wouldn't give for a trip to my club right now, he mused. *Some time in the steam room would be perfect.*

"I wish I could take a hot bath," Carly said just then, echoing his fantasy. "Wouldn't that be heavenly?"

"Heavenly, all right."

She glanced at him wryly. "Okay, you don't have to be sarcastic."

"I wasn't!"

"I'll admit I'm not exactly a nature girl."

I'm not exactly delighted with our circumstances, either, Hank wanted to say. *There's nothing I like better than a luxury hotel—preferably within walking distance of a good museum, a decent neighborhood bar and a ballpark.* But a clap of thunder prevented him from saying so aloud.

Carly sighed pensively, listening to the rain. "I remember getting caught in a storm like this in London once."

"What happened?"

She smiled dreamily and settled back against the saddle. "I was with an old girlfriend. To get out of the rain, we ducked into a spa near Kensington Palace. We had our nails done, facials, new makeup. They gave us herbal tea and little shortbread cookies—it was wonderful. Afterward, we went to the theater—the perfect ending to a perfect day.''

''Sounds great,'' Hank said, completely truthful.

''I love being pampered.''

Hank liked the way Carly looked just then—happily daydreaming about creature comforts and the pleasures of civilization. Hank wanted to counter with a story of his own favorite day spent in London—starting with an afternoon punting on the Thames River with an attractive Englishwoman who wrote for the *London Times,* then dinner at a terrific Indian restaurant where the waiters spoke not a single word of English and finally a rock concert patronized by some very lovely members of the royal family. He'd been in England for a hiking tour, but Hank was willing to bet Carly would have enjoyed every moment of that day he'd spent in London, too.

But he roused himself to play the cowboy one more time. ''Well, we have cold coffee,'' he said cheerfully. ''And at least half a sandwich to share.''

He reached for the thermos and unfastened the lid. Pouring cold coffee a moment later, he said, ''Tell me about other trips you've taken.''

''Oh, you wouldn't find them very interesting, I'm afraid.'' She sounded depressed. ''I like museums and concert halls and musty old bookshops.''

What I wouldn't give to be in a musty old bookshop right now, he thought wistfully. But he said, ''What are your favorite bookstores?''

The subject was obviously near and dear to Carly's heart. She pulled herself together and was soon rhapsodizing about shops in cities all over the world, told him about first-edition volumes she'd found in Rome and a complete set of Jane Austen novels in a lovely old shop in Edinburgh. There was a shop that served iced coffee in Istanbul and another in Greece that opened into a small café on a rear courtyard. Listening to her made Hank want to visit each and every spot she mentioned.

Carly did a great deal of traveling, Hank decided. Some of it was business, but mostly she visited faraway places for pleasure. She sometimes traveled alone, sometimes with friends. He caught a hint that she once took a trip with a gentleman friend, but it hadn't turned out well.

"It sounds like you do the calendar business just to finance your travels," he observed.

Carly looked guilty for an instant, then smiled. "I suppose so. I don't exactly love my work, but it allows me to pay hotel bills."

"Why don't you try something else?" he suggested. "Find some work you'd love to do."

"Oh, my life's not about work," Carly said firmly. "I enjoy too many things to tie myself to a desk."

"Besides travel, books and theater—what else?"

"I write a little. Nothing published, of course. I volunteer at a retirement village two Saturdays a month."

"Doing what?"

"Mostly driving nice ladies to do their shopping. My parents moved there a couple of years ago. My mother passed away, but Dad's still playing bridge with his friends every morning and hitting a few golf balls every afternoon."

"You spend a lot of time with him?"

"My sisters and I have dinner with him once every week or so, but he's busy with his pals. Mostly I go to visit with the ladies. I love listening to their stories. One of these days I'm going to put a bunch of them into a book."

"Sounds like a good idea," Hank said.

"I think it would make my mom proud."

"Maybe you ought to do some travel writing, too."

"Who needs another travel writer?" she asked rhetorically, shaking her head as though it were a lost cause.

The paper I work for needs somebody, Hank thought. *Not full-time, but writing on commission would earn a lot of frequent flyer miles.*

"Besides," she said before he could ask her to talk more about her writing, "I'm comfortable doing what I do with the calendars. Not delighted, but comfortable."

And Carly liked her comforts, Hank decided, but he also decided to learn more about this part of her life later.

The conversation meandered for a while, gradually circling back to family. Carly delicately pressed for a few more details about Hank's life.

"Your parents must have started this ranch," she said, opening a new subject.

"My great-grandparents, actually. They came here from Boston and started the ranch from nothing."

"No wonder you want to hang on to the land."

"Well, not all of us do."

She tilted her head. "What do you mean?"

"Becky runs the—I mean, Becky and I run the place, but my parents are still alive. They moved to Florida a few years ago."

Her eyes widened. "Oh, I just assumed they had passed away."

"Nope. They just hated farming. At least, my mother did. And when Dad broke his legs two years in a row, she convinced him it was time to get off the horses and onto the beaches. He wasn't hard to convince."

"How did your parents meet?"

"They grew up side by side. Mom's family has a general store a few miles down the road."

"A few miles?"

"Well, forty," Hank said with a smile. "Distances are measured differently here."

"So I've noticed. Forty miles is considered living side by side, hmm?"

"Yep. They went to school together and married at eighteen. Mom knew what she was getting into, but she never really liked being a rancher's wife and quit after twenty-five years."

Hank did not add his mother had been the one—frantic to escape the ranch herself—who encouraged her son to go east for schooling and a career. Becky had been born to ranching, but young Henry's destiny had been different. Reading, writing and traveling had luckily combined into a lucrative career that Hank wouldn't trade for anything. He had his mother to thank for that, he knew.

Carly said, "Your parents left recently?"

"Four or five years ago. Working the ranch has

always been a struggle, but since they left it's been even tougher.''

''But you must love it.''

''Well—''

''I can see that you're a man with strong feelings and loyalties. Your roots must be important to you.''

''I've always thought,'' he said slowly, ''that a person had to be strong enough to put down his roots wherever he went. Would you like that sandwich now?''

Close call, Hank thought. He could see that Carly was still enamored of the mythic cowboy baloney. And he realized that she was ready to pay Becky the ten thousand just to keep her romantic notions alive. *Better not screw up Becky's chances.*

He felt a little rotten about keeping the truth from Carly—a sentiment that grew throughout the evening as she told him more bits and pieces of her life.

He heard about her sisters, both younger, who had three children between them and enjoyed life in the California suburbs. She also talked about her partner Bert, who sounded like a jerk to Hank, but he kept his opinions to himself. He suspected Carly's relationship with her partner had not always been totally business.

They talked for a couple of hours without pause, getting to know each other little by little.

When the rain eased up, they ventured to put their noses outside the tent. Half to himself, Hank said, ''We should try walking now. The moon may come out soon.''

The night was black and cold, and the moon did

not appear. Carly shuddered. "Is it really safe walking back on a night like this?"

Hank hated to think of a long, wet hike, too. "Maybe it will be safer if we stay here."

Carly shifted her weight and winced. "I should have cleaned up the rocks better before we put the tent here."

She *had* managed to choose a very uncomfortable spot for their shelter. Not only was the ground hard, cold and rocky, but Hank didn't like the sight of the creek rising quickly toward them.

"Maybe we'd better move to higher ground," he suggested.

Carly looked alarmed. "Are we going to be flooded?"

"No, no," Hank lied. "But the noise of the creek might keep us awake."

Carly frowned as if she didn't believe him. She helped Hank pack up their few belongings and shift everything to a different location. The work was made more difficult by darkness and a biting wind.

The second spot Carly chose was almost as bad as the first, and the tent collapsed into a heap as they moved it. Hank doggedly reassembled the damned thing and held back colorful curses while he worked. When they reentered the tent, they were both short-tempered, cold and tired.

"We should have started back sooner," Carly said, bumping into Hank in the dark.

He bumped her back. "We were otherwise occupied."

"I'm not blaming you." She sounded touchy.

"I didn't think you were."

"Your tone—"

"Don't bite my head off."

"Let's get some sleep." Carly handed Hank one of the blankets. "Or try to, at least."

They wrapped up in separate blankets and lay down in the darkness just as the rain started again. Somehow, the sound of rain made their situation even more miserable.

Beneath them, the ground was unforgiving and damp. The tent was leaning dangerously in the wind and threatened to blow over any moment. The whole world was cold and noisy. Hank's stomach growled.

But there was no food, no heat, nothing to talk about anymore. Nothing to do until morning—and that was hours away.

Beside him, Carly was silent and motionless, but it was easy to sense that she felt exactly the way he did. Never had either one of them been so miserable in all their lives.

But suddenly a thought made the miserableness even more complete.

There *was* something they could do to keep their minds off their troubles. Carly's warm body was just a touch away. Her clothes could come off in a trice, Hank thought. He almost groaned at the thought of how she might feel, slipping into his arms again. His imagination conjured up images of how they could spend a breathless night together.

But they lacked one important thing.

If only, Hank thought, *we had a condom.*

Six

Carly had never spent a worse night in her life. Not only was she horribly uncomfortable, but her brain seemed permanently fogged with sexual fantasies concerning Hank Fowler.

And she woke up thinking she never wanted to see him again.

Oh, it wasn't that she wasn't attracted to the man. Or that she didn't like him. Frankly, he was the sexiest and perhaps the sweetest man she'd ever met. And he'd managed to wrap himself around her during the night and even slipped his hand under her shirt so that he had warmly cupped Carly's right breast in a deliciously unconscious way.

God help me, she thought, *but I want to roll over, strip off his clothes and make love to him here and now.*

But there was no way in hell they'd ever have a future together.

I hate the outdoors, she told herself. *There's no use denying it.*

Even if he was God's gift to women everywhere, the fact that he lived in the middle of a wasteland rendered Hank Fowler the last man she'd ever start a relationship with.

Not after yesterday and last night.

Just my luck. I find Mr. Right and it turns out he owns several hundred acres that would make a grizzly bear weep.

Nevertheless, Carly enjoyed the heat that radiated from his lean body. Her bottom was intimately snuggled against him, and one of his long legs rode comfortably between her knees. She could feel his breath—even and deep—whispering along her hairline. Remembering the heart-pounding way they'd explored each other's bodies yesterday, Carly flushed warmly. When had she ever allowed a man to touch her the way Hank had?

We certainly got to know each other fast.

And yet Carly couldn't help feeling Hank was holding something back.

She wanted to know him completely. But not at the risk of dying in the wilderness, she decided.

I'm taking the first plane back to Los Angeles. Somehow, I've got to forget this man.

Hank woke up then and groaned.

"You okay?" Carly asked, not moving from his embrace. He sounded as if he were in pain.

"Hell," he muttered. "What train hit me?"

"What's wrong?" Carly sat up quickly, jostling Hank in the process.

"Ow, don't!" He cringed as if she'd run over him with a bulldozer. "Jeez, I'm dying."

Hank opened his eyes and looked startled to find Carly staring at him. It took a moment for reality to settle in, then he said blankly, "Oh, it's you."

The lack of romance in his tone stung her pride. "Maybe you were expecting Pocahontas in this charming teepee?"

Hank sat up cautiously, holding his head as if to keep his wits from swirling around. "Man, that was a rough night, wasn't it?"

"Are you in pain?"

"Agony," he corrected. "I think every bone in my body is broken."

"I think you slept on a rock."

He rubbed his back. "That explains my ruptured kidney."

"Can you stand up?"

"No," he said. "I think I'll just wait here for the rescue helicopter."

"Hank—"

"I'm joking," he soothed. Slowly he raised himself to a sitting position, but Hank didn't look any healthier than he had a few moments ago. His face showed a liberal growth of beard, gray circles under his bleary blue eyes and distinct grooves that ran from his nose to the corners of his mouth.

Carly couldn't hold back a grin. "Boy, you look a little worse for wear. What happened? Did a prairie dog beat you up during the night?"

"I'm not the only one looking less than perfect."

Carly's spine snapped straight. "What's that sup-posed to mean?"

"Just—oh, nothing. Sorry."

Steaming, Carly let herself out of the tent and into the feeble rays of early sunshine. Her sneakers squished in the soft ground as she walked away from the tent, smoothing her hair and pinching her cheeks to bring back their color.

"Hey, wait," Hank called, gingerly pulling him-self out of the tent. "Carly!"

"I'm going to wash my face," she snapped. "Ap-parently, I need it."

"I didn't mean anything by—ow, dammit!"

Hank continued to curse as he tried climbing to his feet, joints and bones making little cracking noises, but Carly stalked away from him, thoroughly annoyed.

"Okay, so I don't look like Cleopatra this morn-ing," she muttered, putting a hundred yards between them. "Did he have to point it out?"

Of course, nothing had stopped Carly from making the observation that Hank hadn't exactly been his most attractive.

She knelt at the edge of the muddy, storm-swollen stream and swished her hands in the cold water. The shock of the cold made her fingers ache in seconds. Looking at her hands, Carly moaned. "Brother, do I need a manicure! Probably a facial, too."

She rubbed her face and found it rough and sun-burned. With a little water, she tried smoothing her hair into place. But it was probably a lost cause.

A noise made Carly look up from her ablutions, and she found herself staring into the slanted green eyes of Baby, the pup. Two yards away, the animal was crouched behind a rock and peeking at her.

"Good morning, sweetheart," she cooed, holding out her fingers to the pup. "Want to be friends again?"

The pup was shy this morning, but not as hostile as she had been the night before. With some coaxing, Carly managed to catch the wolf and hug it tightly against her chest. She returned to their pathetic campsite with the pup in her arms.

"Oh, no," groaned Hank, looking up from the sodden remains of their fire. "You found it again."

"Of course I did. She's too young to be on her own out here. She needs us."

Hank seemed on the brink of arguing, but they were interrupted at that moment by the sounds of approaching horses. Climbing onto the highest nearby rock, Hank waved and shouted, "Becky! Over here!"

Carly had never been so relieved in her life as she was when Becky Fowler and another cowboy rode into the campsite, leading Laverne and Buttercup behind their own horses.

"Hi, guys," Becky called cheerfully. "That was some storm last night, wasn't it?"

"You bet," Hank replied, sounding not very friendly. "Were you safe and warm?"

"Of course, Hank. Chet built a fire in the fireplace, and we had grilled steaks with onions and some of that wine you brought from—"

"I'm glad you enjoyed yourselves," Hank said, cutting her off. "Hello, Chet."

The cowboy named Chet had reined his magnificent Appaloosa horse and comfortably leaned one elbow on the horn of his saddle to look down at Hank. He was a tall, thin young man about Becky's age, with a beaten-up cowboy hat and an old oilskin coat over his jeans and flannel shirt. His face was leathery tan beneath a pair of reflecting sunglasses that perched on his hawklike nose. Carly thought he looked vastly amused as he smiled down at Hank.

"Hey, there, Henry," he drawled. "You get yourself into a little trouble?"

"Nothing we couldn't survive," Hank shot back, with a smile that looked as cold as Chet's. "Nice of you to bring our horses back."

"No trouble at all," Chet replied. "Think you can ride this bronco home?"

Hank snatched Buttercup's reins from Chet's gloved hand and said nothing.

Becky dismounted and turned to Carly with concern on her face. "I hope you weren't too uncomfortable last night. The storm was— What in the world is that?"

"A wolf." Carly turned so that Becky could look into the pup's face. "We found her mother over there—shot dead. This little girl wouldn't have lived long if we hadn't found her."

"Uh—exactly what were you planning on doing with it?" Becky asked carefully. "It's a wild animal, you know."

"We can't just leave it to die!"

But one glance around at the three faces that stared at her and Carly knew that Becky, Chet and Hank could easily leave the little pup to die. In fact, they clearly expected *her* to drop Baby that instant and ride home to the ranch without a backward glance.

Carly's temper rose. "I'm not leaving her behind, you know. She needs food and protection."

"But—" Becky started to protest.

"But—" Hank began.

"Aw," said Chet, "I think you're kinda cute together. Howdy, ma'am. I'm Chet Roswell. I own a few acres north of here."

"I'm delighted to meet you, Chet." Carly shifted Baby's weight and stuck her hand up for Chet to shake. "Are you volunteering to help me?"

Becky and Hank swung on him, but Chet was laughing. "Sure thing, ma'am. Want me to carry the little feller?"

"I'd be very appreciative."

"Now that we've got *that* settled," Hank said testily, "why don't we break camp and get home to a hot shower?"

"Too bad there's not a Jacuzzi back at the ranch," Chet said laconically. "Henry looks like he could use a hot soak."

Becky shot Chet a quelling glance, but he laughed uproariously as if he'd cracked a hilarious joke.

It didn't take long to clean up the tent and blankets, and Carly was glad to find herself en route to the ranch within a few moments. Relieved that Chet had volunteered to take Baby, she concentrated on making her stiff muscles hold her steady in Laverne's saddle. The ride took less than an hour, but Carly's aching body protested every step Laverne took.

The only bright spot in her morning was noticing

that Hank looked every bit as uncomfortable as she did.

Back at the ranch, Carly thankfully turned Laverne over to one of the visiting ranch hands and was glad that Chet offered to make a pen for Baby. She put the pup out of her mind and limped over to the house. A shower. A bed. That's all she wanted. She climbed the front steps with clenched teeth, trying not to cry out when her legs protested the stairs.

The bathtub was a delight. Carly soaked for twenty minutes after swallowing two aspirin. When she emerged from the bathroom, Becky called up the stairs to her.

"You had a phone call from your office last night, Carly. From a man who called himself Bert. He asked you to call back today."

"Thanks," Carly said faintly. "I'll call him and go to bed for a while, if that's okay?"

"Sure. Hank's on the phone at the moment, but he won't be more than a couple of minutes. I've got some errands to do, but I'll be back in a few hours. Hank can get you anything you need."

"Thanks."

Carly found her lightweight bathrobe and put it on before descending the stairs in search of the phone. Hank was standing in the kitchen, and he hung up the receiver just as she walked in. Carly wondered if he'd cut his call short when he'd heard her approach.

"It's all yours," he said, attempting to sound cheerful. "And there are biscuits and bacon in the warmer, if you're hungry. Want some coffee?"

"That would be wonderful."

While Carly dialed the 800 number of the Twilight

offices, Hank pulled a thick mug from a shelf and poured it full of steaming black coffee for her. Moving slowly—as if in pain—he prepared her breakfast. He got jam and butter from the refrigerator and left them on the table within Carly's reach. As soon as her call connected, however, Hank left the kitchen so she could speak privately with Bert.

"Hi," she said when her partner's voice came on the line. "It's me."

"Sounding a little under the weather, too," Bert observed. "You okay?"

"I'll live."

"What's the matter? Did the cowboy prince turn out to be a frog?"

"No, that's not it. Rough night, that's all. I'm longing for the comforts of civilization."

"Anything I can do?"

Carly sighed. "Nothing, I'm afraid."

Bert's voice softened. "Are you disappointed, love?"

It took a long moment for Carly to summon an honest answer. "Not disappointed, no. Tired at the moment. But…"

"Is he everything you expected?"

"Yes. And more, I guess. Oh, it's complicated."

"Complicated?" Bert echoed, laughing. "You've only been gone a couple of days! You're talking like there's a relationship going sour already."

"There *is* no relationship," Carly countered.

"But you'd like one?" Bert inquired archly.

"No. Maybe. Yes, if the geography wasn't so bad." She blew another sigh. "I don't know what I'm saying, Bert. I'm tired and cranky, that's all."

"Well, business can wait in that case."

"No, I'm ready to talk," she said quickly. "What's going on in the office?"

"I've sent a photographer to you. It's Alexis from Marvel Photo—remember her? She'll be arriving tomorrow. Will you have test shots for her by then?"

"I can take them, but I don't think I can have anything developed. This place is in the middle of nowhere, Bert."

"No matter. Alexis does good work—especially if her material is up to snuff."

Carly thought about Hank's stiff limp and exhausted face. "Well, I think it'll be okay."

"Don't worry. We can always touch up in the darkroom."

"Right. Anything else?"

"No—except to make sure you're all right."

"All I need is rest."

"Go to bed, then. Call me later, if you want to talk."

"Okay. Bert…"

He had been ready to hang up, but his voice came back on the line. "Yes?"

"Thanks."

"For what?"

"Being there, I guess."

"Feeling vulnerable, are we?"

"A little."

"Well, be careful. You always get reckless when you're feeling that way."

Carly mustered a laugh. "Don't worry. See you in a few days."

They hung up, and Carly was suddenly starved.

She wolfed down some bacon, two biscuits with jam and drank a quick cup of very hot coffee. After a refill, she carried the mug back up the stairs.

On the landing she encountered Hank who had clearly stepped out from under the shower moments before. He had opened the bathroom door to let out the steam and was brushing his teeth in the doorway, wearing nothing but a blue towel around his hips. And he completely filled the doorway. His hair was wet, and water clung to his chest. His eyelashes and mustache were thickened with droplets, too. Even undressed, he looked every inch a sexy cowboy.

He stopped brushing his teeth and looked around at Carly with something odd flickering in his blue eyes. With a jolt Carly realized it was the same expression that had been captured in the original photograph she'd received—the photo Carly had kept at her bedside.

For a moment Carly was speechless. His gaze reflected warmth and humor and something more sensual. Something very male, magnetic and knowing.

Carly's imagination took a dive back into yesterday's wildly abandoned encounter under the warm sun. No doubt Hank was thinking exactly the same thing. She felt a blush start on her cheekbones and suddenly wished she'd put on some underwear beneath her bathrobe.

"Uh," she said, when she could make her wits function. "Going to bed?"

Hank nodded, his mouth full of toothbrush. "You?"

"Yes, I'm—well, after last night—"

"Tired?"

"I…I was. But the coffee." She tried to summon a smile as she lifted the mug in her hand. "Becky makes pretty strong stuff, doesn't she?"

Hank turned away, spat in the sink and rinsed his mouth. Then, grabbing another towel, he came out onto the landing where Carly stood. He leaned one bare shoulder against the doorjamb and buffed his wet hair with the extra towel. "Yeah, I had a cup myself."

"So," she said, holding her ground just six inches from him. "You're not very tired right now, either?"

"Not very."

"Then…"

"Yes?"

"We—I mean— Maybe a few things need to be said."

"You're right." He stopped drying his hair. "Listen, about what I said this morning. It was stupid. I wasn't thinking. I'm sorry I hurt your feelings."

"Oh, that was nothing. I was too touchy. I slept badly, and I was hungry—"

"You looked great," he said softly.

Suddenly Carly felt as if her brains had turned to mush. "What?"

A ghost of a grin appeared at one corner of his wonderful mouth, and his gaze seemed to pierce Carly's soul. "Really, you did. You woke up looking very…desirable. A little ruffled around the edges, but you have the most incredible blue, bedroom eyes."

"I do?"

"And," he said, leaning imperceptibly closer, "you look even better right now."

Carly's mouth got very dry, and she couldn't think

of a blessed thing to say. She stood on the landing, holding a cup of coffee and waiting shakily as Hank leaned closer and closer and closer.

Hank heard alarm bells going off in his head. Every brain cell that was still functioning told him to stop, stop, stop. But the rest of his body was completely ignoring the warning signs, and something instinctive was taking over.

She looked so lovely at that moment. A little dazed, a little flushed from her bath. Her short hair was still delightfully rumpled. And underneath that filmy little robe, she was completely naked, no doubt about it.

Hank quit thinking and kissed her. He found her mouth with his and slipped one hand into the soft fringe of blond hair at the back of her neck. Under his thumb, he felt her pulse quicken. At that, a slow rush of sexual desire flooded his system, and he deepened the kiss to something much more demanding.

Carly resisted for a fraction of a second, her right arm rigidly extended to prevent the coffee from spilling. She froze, but then Hank felt her lips soften against his. And in another heartbeat, she was pressing against him, aligning her slim body to fit against Hank. She slid her free hand up his arm and around his shoulder, lifting up on tiptoe to match the intensity of his kiss. They didn't breathe, didn't think. Just melded in a quiet, delicious moment.

But then she drew back. Gently. Turning her head away so that he couldn't see her eyes, Carly stopped the kiss and took a deep, steadying breath. Hank held her close, unwilling to let her body part from his.

"I had decided to stop this," she whispered, her face turned away. "Before it went any farther."

"Stop what?"

"This," she said. "This *thing* between us. This sex thing."

"What's wrong?"

"Nothing. Oh, Hank." She began to quiver in his arms. At first it was very slight, but gradually her whole body was trembling against his.

"Hey," he murmured, his lips against her temple. "Hey, easy now."

"I shouldn't be kissing you."

"Why not? We're consenting adults."

"But," she said, "we're not going to have anything else, are we? A relationship, I mean. It's just going to be a good time. A one-night stand."

"Well—"

"It makes me sad, that's all. I like you, Hank. I actually think we could be good together." She looked up at last, her gaze teary.

She's right, Hank thought. *We could be very good together. And not just in bed. We're a lot alike.*

"But," Carly went on raggedly, "I've come to an important realization. I've learned something about myself."

"What's that?"

"That I hate the country!" She choked, and suddenly the tears were spilling down her cheeks. "I am a city person, Hank. I thought a ranch would be romantic and...and...wonderful, but it isn't. It's uncomfortable and inconvenient and...and...I want to go home."

Amen! Hank wanted to shout. But he took the coffee cup from her hand and steered Carly into her bedroom. He kicked the door closed behind them and guided her gently down onto the bed where she proceeded to dissolve into great, gulping sobs.

"I'm so ashamed of myself," she went on. "I'm such a coward and a feeble, weak—"

"No, you're not." Hank sat down beside her and set the mug of coffee on the window ledge. "You're anything but weak."

"I loved the scenery, but I'm just not cut out to *live* in it. Do you understand?"

Unable to hold back a smile, Hank said, "More than you know." He smoothed her hair back from her face. He kissed her wet cheek. "It's nothing to cry about, Carly."

"But...but...I *like* you. Yesterday was—it was good, wasn't it?"

"Better than good."

She hiccuped. "And now I just want to hold you and— Oh, hell, why not say it? I want to make love with you for hours. Isn't that crazy?"

His lips had found her jawline, and Hank began tracing its length with feathery kisses. "Crazy? No. Maybe an idea worth trying, though."

"It's wanton or something."

"It's *nice*. Makes me feel..."

She used the fingers of her left hand to stroke his face. "How?"

He grinned. "Like making love for hours."

"You don't think I'm some kind of horrible hussy?"

He couldn't stop a laugh. "Hussy?"

"You know what I mean."

"Carly," he said patiently, "I'm a guy. In a situation like this, I think you're anything but horrible. In fact, I'll nominate you for goddess status if you'll let me take this robe off."

She laughed unsteadily and closed her eyes. "I want to pretend we're in a lovely penthouse suite with room service just a phone call away and my manicurist just a block down the street and—"

"What about a steam room?"

"Do you like steam rooms?"

"Love 'em," Hank mumbled, his lips moving down her soft throat.

"Is it like a sauna?"

"Yep."

"I...I like saunas."

He had the tie of her robe in one hand and tugged it loose. Without pause, he skimmed kisses across her collarbone and down the smooth skin of her chest. He could feel her heart leap beneath her breast as his lower lip made contact with the nipple. It bloomed against his mouth, and Hank couldn't hold back an incoherent mutter.

Carly sighed and arched her back involuntarily. "Maybe we should just live for the moment, especially since Becky's away doing some errands."

"Once in a while," he murmured between swipes of his tongue, "living for the moment...is a good thing."

She laced her fingers in his hair and held Hank's head. "Ohh, that's wonderful."

"This?"

She blew another long sigh. "Oh, Hank."

Carly eased down on the bed, drawing Hank with

her until they were stretched out on the bedclothes together. The bed made a quiet sound under them. Lying there was definitely more comfortable than on a blanket spread out over rocky ground, Hank thought with pleasure. And Carly felt soft and curvy beneath his hands, more potent than wine beneath his lips.

Hank slid out of his towel. Carly arched out of her robe, and he rode into the curve of her body. The friction of their bare skin was almost more than Hank could stand.

Carly smoothed her hands around his shoulders, across his back. Her fingertips traced dizzying designs on his back.

"Another minute and I won't be able to stop," he whispered, nuzzling her softness. "Are you sure about this?"

"Oh, yes." Her thighs parted. "I can't wait any longer."

"Then I've got to go back to my room for a second. I think I've got a condom—"

"There's one in my suitcase," she said with a smile that was half ashamed, half pleased with herself. "I checked before I took my shower."

Hank laughed, liking her very much. He stretched for her nearby suitcase and dragged it closer to the bed. Turning over on her side, Carly reached over the edge of the bed and flipped open the case. She rummaged for only a second before coming up with a foil packet. By that time Hank had begun to nibble the back of her neck.

In another moment they were tumbling on the bed. Carly's caresses were erotic, her kisses playful. She laughed in the back of her throat when Hank made his desires clear, and shortly he was out of his head with the sensual games she could play with her mouth.

They didn't take much time to explore or tease, however. There was more urgency in Carly's whispers than there had been yesterday. More tension sang in the muscles of her body. Hank obeyed her wishes and soon found himself poised and ready above her.

"Now," she murmured. She told Hank in breathless phrases exactly what she wanted, and he sank inside her with a single thrust that was more powerful than he intended. Carly eagerly rose to meet him, though, and shuddered with pleasure when he was deeply inside. Her eyes were alight, her mouth curved in a warm smile.

Looking down at her, Hank felt a pang of emotion in his heart. She felt so good, so perfect. For him, it was as if he'd come home—not to a ranch, but to woman. The right woman at long last.

He wanted to tell her that. He wanted to say the words, to explain everything. But she was too exciting, too insistent, too aroused. Carly wrapped her long legs around his hips, holding him inside her as she settled her shoulders firmly into the bed. Then she arched upward and began to rock. Languidly at first. Then with greater passion.

She was molten lava, and Hank moved with the deep waves she created. Beautiful, powerful sensations washed over him like ocean surf. He tried, but he couldn't hold back the urge to quicken the tempo, to strengthen his thrusts.

Carly gasped, but met each of the thrusts with growing abandon. The rhythm grew, mounting steadily. Thrust after thrust. Cry after cry. Hank lost all sense of time and space. He forgot to be gentle.

At last Carly shuddered powerfully. She gasped his name and opened her eyes wide. Hank drank in their expression. He saw the ecstasy that boiled over inside her. And the emotion. She cried out and quivered beneath him, and Hank felt his soul implode at the same instant. Together they were suddenly suspended in the universe.

Then the world burst into a thousand stars.

Hank had Carly wrapped in his arms. She was wound around him like a delicate wraith. For a long time, that was all he knew. They seemed to float back to reality with the same drifting speed as a wind-blown leaf returning to earth.

He rolled onto his side, drawing Carly with him so that they lay for a long time with noses touching. Carly's smile was warm and sleepy. Hank knew he probably looked just the same way—exhausted and satisfied.

No words were needed.

But he murmured, "Where have you been all my life?"

Warmed by his words, Carly closed her eyes and listened to Hank's breathing steady and gradually get long and relaxed. He fell asleep a little while later, leaving her alone with her thoughts.

What had attracted her to this man in the first place? The way he looked—tall, lean and handsome with his Marlboro Man mustache and heavenly shoulders? Or his easy laugh, the calm drawl in his voice? The sometimes wicked gleam in his sky blue eyes?

No, perhaps it had been something even less obvious that appealed to Carly at first.

A cowboy came with fewer complications than a man from the real world in L.A., Carly thought. He ought to be easy to get along with. He didn't come with a lot of excess baggage. He rode his horse, drove a rattletrap pickup truck while listening to country-western music, looked after his cattle and didn't worry about issues that plagued the rest of the world. The fantasy man had spun around in Carly's imagination for weeks. She had his personality created before she knew him.

But is that Hank? Carly frowned to herself. *Is he the fantasy cowboy I dreamed up?*

Maybe not, she reasoned. He wasn't a cardboard cutout of a man. He wasn't shallow and empty-headed.

He was real. With a sometimes short temper, an intolerance of discomfort, an easy way of finding out about Carly's life and family. He was smart and capable, not to mention definitely an accomplished lover. It was hard to believe he'd lived all his life isolated on a South Dakota ranch, especially given some of the references he'd made on their camping trip.

But suddenly Carly's brain was too fogged to puzzle through that thought. She dozed off, smiling.

Seven

Lust isn't love, Carly told herself the following day. *But it certainly feels the same sometimes.*

Her entire being felt consumed by Hank Fowler. She even forgot to wish for cigarettes. One addiction had been traded for another, and this one was wonderfully tempting.

The day had dawned sunny and cool, perfect weather for working in the corral, Becky had declared at breakfast, giving her brother a stern eye.

Carly spent some time with Chet Roswell learning how to care for Baby, but her mind wasn't really able to concentrate. Not with Hank floating in and out of her imagination as frequently as he did. She found herself looking over her shoulder every few minutes to see what Hank was doing on the other side of the corral.

"That's it, ma'am," Chet coaxed. "You hold that bottle with your right hand and the little sweetheart in your left arm. Here, let me—yeah, that's right as rain. Later on, we'll give her some solid food, too."

"Thanks, Chet. I appreciate your help."

"Oh, sugar pie, I'd do anything to help out a cute little lady like you."

Normally Carly would have thrown a temper tantrum at any man who called her a cute little anything. But Carly hardly listened to a word Chet said to her.

Across the corral, however, Hank was in a very different mood.

"Who does that slime bucket think he is, touching her like that?"

Becky looked up from the calf she was trying to examine for signs of blindness. "Will you hold that rope steady, please, Henry? And hug his neck tighter. I don't want to get my toes broken because you're too busy keeping an eagle eye on your girlfriend."

Hank gripped the small calf as snugly as he could. "She's not my girlfriend. And she's certainly not his, either!"

"What have you got against Chet?"

Hank tried to hold the struggling calf as Becky had instructed, but he couldn't help glancing over his shoulder at Carly, who seemed engrossed in every nuance that Chet was preaching about. She didn't shrug off Chet's hand when he held her arm. "I haven't got anything against Roswell."

"You've hated his guts since elementary school," Becky returned.

"He used to bully everybody in Miss Hardwick's third-grade class," Hank mumbled.

"Wait a minute. I thought *you* were the one who got kicked out of that third-grade class."

"For punching Chet Roswell," Hank snapped. "I couldn't take it anymore. He was picking on Julie Goodman."

"Oh-ho, Julie Goodman!" Becky laughed. "The tough girl with the stubby pigtails. Who could forget her? You always had a soft spot where she was concerned, and I never understood that. Julie was *mean*."

"Not mean, just a girl who knew her own mind."

"She owns a car dealership now."

"Good for her."

"And now you've got a soft spot for Carly. Why? She doesn't need protecting, either."

"I guess I like strong women."

"So you can have a worthy opponent when it comes to stubbornness. Okay, turn him loose. I'll have the vet check him on Friday." Becky dusted off her gloves and watched the freed calf go bounding back to his mama. "Don't you like Chet Roswell at all, Henry?"

"No."

Becky squinted up at him in the sunshine. "Why not?"

"Because he's everything I was supposed to be," Hank said, unable to stop a laugh. "He's a big dumb cowboy who never read a book, but slept with his horse at least once a week. Pop always liked having Chet around—so did you, for that matter, if I remember correctly."

"I still like having him around," Becky said, sounding strange.

Hank took her elbow and spun his sister around so that he could gauge her expression. She looked away quickly. He raised one eyebrow, releasing her arm. "What's that supposed to mean, exactly?"

"Nothing. Well, maybe something." Becky took the rope from him and strolled to the fence. "He's been coming around these past few months. He lost his own ranch a couple of years ago, you know."

"He's a lousy businessman?"

"No, just bad luck, I think. Now he's—well—he's changed, Henry."

"What do you mean? He's not tormenting little girls anymore?"

"I'm not saying Chet doesn't have faults. He has a lot. He's immature and competitive—but we're working on those things."

"We?"

"Chet and I."

Hank saw the truth at last and exploded. "Oh, hell, Becky, you're not going to marry him, are you?"

Becky's swift upward gaze was flinty. "What's it to you if I did?"

Hank caught the words that nearly escaped his mouth. He didn't want to hurt Becky—certainly not because of a childhood relationship that hadn't mattered much to him. One look at Becky's face told him that she had come to know Chet Roswell better in the years since Hank had left the ranch. Surely Chet had grown up. If so, there had to be a way for Hank to put the past behind them.

He mustered a wry grin. "Oh, great. You're going to force me to spend every holiday with the guy who got me kicked out of the third grade—the class with the prettiest teacher in the whole school?''

Becky laughed. ''So, that was it! You were show-ing off for Miss Hardwick all along!''

Hank draped his arm across Becky's shoulders. ''Listen, Beck, if you really want to marry Chester Roswell, go ahead. I'll even come to the wedding and give you matching saddles for a wedding pres-ent. He's not so bad.''

Becky stretched up and kissed Hank's cheek. ''If he leaves your girlfriend alone, you mean?''

''She's not my—''

''Yeah, sure. Don't lie to me, Henry.'' Becky climbed the fence easily, tossing her taunts down at her brother. ''You two were making goo-goo eyes at each other all last evening and this morning, too. And if you want to keep your sleeping arrangements a secret, you'll have to work a little harder. Your bed hasn't been slept in.''

''Oh, jeez.''

Sitting astride the fence, Becky said, ''You could have done worse, you know. I like her a lot. And not just because she's going to give us a bushel of money. She's fun.''

''Yeah,'' Hank admitted. ''I know.''

''And thoughtful. I liked the story she told us last night about her father's travel agency.''

''Yeah, she's funny.''

''And she had you going on politics, too. I never heard you argue like that before. She had you on the ropes, Mr. Columnist.''

Hank remembered Carly's heated argument with a grin. If she could hold her own in a political debate with Henry Fowler, she was made of sterner stuff than most women.

"And she's good-looking," Becky continued. "What are you waiting for, Henry?"

"Maybe it's just a fling."

Becky gave an unladylike snort.

"Okay," Hank said more seriously, "I've got a life somewhere else, that's why. So does she. It's complicated."

"What about that phone call you had yesterday. It was your editor, right? What did he want?"

Hank shot an amused glance up at his sister. "You must have pressed him for a few details when he first called."

"A few," Becky admitted. "He says your column has been sold to a few more papers and there's interest in a big syndication deal. You're expanding into a whole new region. That sounds big."

"It is," Hank said. "It also means travel, lots of changes. I can't just cover Seattle and the Northwest anymore. They want me to start doing resorts and country inns in California and ski resorts in Utah and Idaho. Who knows what else."

"Henry, that's wonderful!"

Hank shook his head. "I'm not so sure. I'm not really a mainstream kind of writer, sis. I'm the grouchy guy who complains about politics and whatever occurs to me, and I—well, gallivanting around posh wine country and spiffy resorts isn't exactly my cup of tea."

"I'll bet you can put your own stamp on the idea, though."

"They want somebody to check out bike trails, white-water rafting, golf courses—"

"Mountains, too?"

"I could probably squeeze in some climbing."

"Wow."

"Yeah," he admitted. "It's the kind of outdoor stuff I enjoy."

"I think you could do it all with the Henry Fowler flavor."

"Maybe," he said pensively. "I'm thinking about it."

"And Carly might fit into your plans somehow."

"We've got a few things to straighten out first."

"Such as?"

There were a great many things Hank wanted to discuss with Carly, but there would be plenty of time for that. First, however, he needed to tell her the truth about his own life and why he'd been keeping it a secret from her.

The longer he waited, the worse it all felt to him. But he put on a cheerful front for Becky.

"Such as nothing you need to worry about," Hank replied, giving her bandanna an affectionate tug.

"Have it your way." Becky tousled Hank's hair and gazed across the corral. "What do you suppose Chet is telling Carly right now?"

Hank looked in the same direction and saw Chet talking faster than a steer could bolt out of a rodeo chute. Something on Carly's face gave Hank a moment's discomfort. She looked decidedly startled. And it wasn't because Chet had his hand on her arm again.

Hank said, "What the hell is he telling her?"

"I can't imagine." Becky swung down from the fence and started to follow Hank across the corral. "Just don't punch him, okay?"

Talking with Chet, Carly learned a few things she didn't comprehend at first.

"It's a great day for riding, Miss Carly."

Feeding time was over, so she put Baby back into the makeshift pen Chet had constructed out of chicken wire. She hardly heard most of what Chet talked about and answered him automatically. "It certainly is."

"How about if I go catch us a couple of horses and saddle up?" He leaned on one of the posts of the pen. "We could mosey out to a little place I know. Maybe you'd like to take a look at the mountains."

"Well, actually, Hank and I are going for a ride later."

"Why, shoot," Chet drawled delightedly. "You might as well go riding with me this afternoon, Miss Carly. Henry's certainly not going to take you out if he can help it. Why, he hates horses more than most men hate shopping."

"What?"

Her expression must have been amusing because Chet began to chuckle. "You didn't notice? Hell, he's practically allergic to 'em. I've never known a man who gets himself thrown off as much as Henry does."

"I thought he was terrific on a horse."

"A carnival pony, maybe!" Chet laughed out loud.

Hank and Becky arrived at that moment, and Carly looked up at Hank with curiosity. He glared at Chet with steel in his eyes.

"What's going on?" Becky asked, looking down into the pen. "Is that pup ready to go back to the wild?"

"Of course not," Carly said at once, forgetting Hank's look and coming to Baby's defense. "She's too young."

"We can't keep her here. She doesn't belong on a ranch."

Carly said, "I'll think of something."

"We'll have the vet look at her when he comes. We have to be careful. She's a wild animal, no matter how cute she looks to you."

Chet laughed. "Miss Carly's just about ready to take this little pup to obedience school."

Becky gave him a quelling glance. "Chet, how about if you give me a hand moving those calves to another field?"

"Sure, honey. Carly says she's goin' ridin' with Henry. Isn't that a laugh?" Chet chortled and put his arm around Becky. Together, they headed back to the corral.

As they departed, Becky could be heard lecturing him in a low, firm voice. Chet defended himself in a whine.

Frowning after them, Carly asked, "What did he mean? I don't think he likes you, Hank."

"Chet and I have a feud going," Hank replied easily, fingering a lock of her hair. "Nothing serious, just a couple of male egos that couldn't stand each other from the moment we looked over the tops of our cribs at each other. How about a walk?''

Carly switched her frown from Chet to Hank and felt a niggle of suspicion start in her mind. But she smiled. ''I thought we were going riding.''

''I've got something to show you instead. Come on.''

They left the main buildings of the ranch and strolled along a fence that ran toward the mountains from the barns. The long grass swished as they walked, and a slight cool breeze ruffled Hank's hair. In the pasture several horses lifted their heads from grazing as they passed.

Carly inhaled the fresh air with newfound pleasure. Then she laughed.

''What's so funny?''

''I've been trying to quit smoking for years. I just realized I haven't even thought about cigarettes for days. This place is good for me, after all.''

As they walked, the scenery seemed to grow more magnificent to Carly—especially since she could keep the Fowler house in sight. She did not want to find herself lost in the wilderness again. The land seemed to expand around her, the horizon slipping farther and farther into the distance.

They walked a mile, perhaps more. The ground rose gradually, and at last Carly realized they had arrived at the top of a long, sloping plateau. From the summit, she thought she could see hundreds of miles in every direction. The sheer distance amazed her. The majesty of those rolling waves of grass took her breath away. She stopped and stood very still, a gasp caught in her throat.

Behind her, Hank said, "Beautiful, isn't it?"

"Wonderful. The grass looks like an ocean."

Hank put his arm around her and pulled Carly back against his chest. "I learned to rock climb up here."

"Really?"

"I graduated to mountains, but this is where it all started."

"You climb mountains? You mean hiking or with axes and cables?"

"The real deal—ice climbing. It scares my mother to death. I'm not world-class, but I love it." He looked out at the vista that sprawled around them. "I used to come up here as a boy and just let my imagination take over."

Carly followed his gaze and leaned back into his frame. "It's hard to believe people actually came across distances like these to make their homes. You must be very proud of your family."

A low laugh vibrated in his chest. "Proud, yes. Sometimes I think they were crazy, too."

"I'm getting the impression you haven't always been in sync with your family."

"Not always," he agreed, then struggled to continue. "We're rooted here, you see, in this beautiful place. But—well, take that pup for instance."

Not sure where the conversation was going, Carly jumped to a conclusion. "She's too young to be set free, Hank. She'll die. Surely you see—"

"I know, I know. But she's meant to be in her natural habitat. We can't change that."

"I don't want her for a pet."

"That's not what I'm talking about, Carly." Hank

turned her around until they were facing each other. His face was set with concentration. "What I mean is, animals aren't like people. Or rather—well—"

She thought he was getting unusually flustered. "What are you trying to say?"

"I love this ranch," Hank went on doggedly, his hands firm on her shoulders. "The land means something to me. It's where my family belongs, and I'm ready to do anything to make sure things stay that way."

"I see," Carly murmured. An awful lump seemed to have sprouted in her throat suddenly. *He's trying to tell me we're finished. We can't be together because he belongs here and I don't.*

He continued speaking, but Carly didn't mentally catch up until he was saying, "Becky's the important factor, you see. The ranch is her life, and I—well, I agreed to help her keep it."

"Uh-huh."

"There's been financial trouble in the past, and Becky needs some serious cash to keep the place going. That's why she entered your contest."

Carly tried to switch mental gears, but her emotions were boiling to the point that not much was making sense. "You'll be getting the ten thousand, I promise."

"That's not what I—"

"Bert found the right photographer. She'll be coming tomorrow, if everything works out. We can take your pictures as soon as she gets here."

Hank blanched and laughed wryly. "I'll have to go through with this, won't I?"

Carly managed a smile. "It'll be a snap. Don't

worry. I won't make you take off your shirt unless you want to."

He laughed. "I *won't* want to!"

"Alexis will make it fun."

"Alexis?" he repeated, feigning dismay. "A woman?"

"Not just one," Carly shot back, amused. "She'll be bringing Rachel, the makeup artist, and probably Deneesa, who does the lighting."

"Oh, God."

"Trust me," Carly soothed with a smile. "They'll be much easier on you than the guys we usually hire. Mark has been known to make grown men weep."

"Carly…"

"Yes?"

Hank held her in his arms and lost himself in the warm gaze she tilted up at him. He loved looking at the sharp planes of her face—the classic curves of her cheekbones, the inquisitive point of her nose, the luscious lips that tasted as delicious as any wine he'd ever enjoyed. The life force that burned behind her eyes was strong enough to make a man forget everything else in the world.

Just looking down at her made Hank's mind go blank.

He gave up trying to explain himself and kissed her instead. A long, sweet kiss that promised much more.

A better time would come, he thought dimly, parting her mouth and delving deep inside. For now, all he wanted was to lose himself in the woman in his arms.

* * *

The following morning, Carly was summoned from her bed by Becky who called through the door that Bert was on the phone again.

"What's going on?" Hank muttered, rolling over when Carly climbed out of the bed and into her robe.

"Go back to sleep," she whispered softly. "I've got a phone call from Bert."

"Kiss me," he commanded in a murmur. "So I won't be jealous."

Touched and amused, she obeyed and tucked him back into the warm bedclothes once again.

Downstairs, Carly picked up the receiver, and said, "This had better be an emergency."

Bert began laughing. "Why? Were you sleeping late? Or otherwise occupied?"

"Never mind," Carly said tartly, but unable to stop smiling. "Don't spoil my mood."

"Boy, you *must* be having a great time," Bert said. "I almost hate to end your vacation."

"Why? What's wrong?"

"A spot of legal trouble, I'm afraid. A bunch of lawyers called from New York, claiming we violated a copyright law with the last calendar. They want half a million dollars, and they're coming to get it."

"What copyright law? Everything was perfectly straight with the photos we used."

"Can you prove that?"

"Yes," Carly said, sure of herself. "I have all the paperwork in a file."

"Is it something I can handle?"

Carly considered the situation. It wasn't the first time some entrepreneurial lawyers came looking to take a cut out of Twilight's profits. She knew this bunch was just fishing, too. There was a good chance Bert could handle the problem, but Bert had been known to drop the ball under pressure.

"When are they coming?"

"They're on a plane right now."

Carly groaned. "A preemptive strike. All right, I'll come as soon as I can make arrangements. You'll have to stall them until I get there."

"When will that be?"

"Before sunset, I hope. Get off the phone and let me call the airlines."

"Carly," said Bert, before she hung up, "thanks. I owe you."

She smiled ruefully. "I'll collect eventually."

Upstairs shortly thereafter, Carly broke the news to a sleepy Hank.

"My plane leaves in six hours. It will take me that long to find the airport."

He woke up fast and caught her wrist, his expression concerned. "Let me drive you."

Pleased that he was ready to help her, Carly shook her head and tried to make her voice sound more cheerful than she was feeling. "I can find the airport by myself. Besides, you're needed here today. Becky tells me the buyers are coming for your cattle. You'll have to be here for that, right?"

"Well—Carly, listen." Hank sat up in bed, his bare chest looking so stunning in the light of day that it was hard for Carly to keep her hands off him. He was serious, though, and said, "There's something you'd better hear from me before you leave."

"Sure," she said, getting up hastily lest the temptation to touch him grew too strong to resist. She began throwing clothes into her suitcase. "But do you mind telling me while I shower? I've got to rush."

Hank sank back into the pillows. "No, that's okay. What I need to explain will have to be spelled out pretty clearly. I'll wait."

Carly swooped down and planted a hot kiss on his mouth. "There. Think of me while I'm in the shower."

He grinned. "You bet."

It was best, Carly thought later on the plane, to leave in a rush. There had been no time for a sappy scene with tears and a lot of stupid promises. Instead, they had parted in a very public spot on the porch with Becky and Chet watching unabashedly.

Deciding a handshake would be silly, Carly started to get into the rented Jeep as quickly as possible. But Hank pulled her back out into the sunlight. "Hold it."

"But—"

He stopped her protest with his mouth, kissing Carly right in front of his sister and Chet. It was a good kiss, too—full of passion and heat.

When he released her, Carly said in a shaky voice, "I guess we're not keeping this a secret anymore?"

"I want to shout it from the top of the weather vane," he replied with an intimate smile, leaning his forehead against hers. "Besides, I think Becky knows everything."

"How did she guess?"

"If I tell you, you'll blush."

Smiling, Carly closed her eyes and tried to commit

to memory every feeling she experienced at that moment. There were too many—all confused, but wonderful. She inhaled a breath and drew away unwillingly.

"Take care of Baby for me," she called as she got into the Jeep.

Yes, a quick departure had been best. Carly had forced herself not to cry by concentrating on driving, then on finding her plane in the airport. Seated on the flight at last, she kept her face turned to the small window and tried to memorize every moment she'd spent with Hank Fowler.

It had felt like lust, she thought. But Carly found herself believing it was love that had grown so quickly between them.

Nothing else could have felt so strong, so magnetic.

The whole way back to L.A., she tried to think of ways she could spend the rest of her life with Hank Fowler. But all her plans seemed to involve blowing up the Fowler ranch.

Eight

An enormous basket of flowers awaited Carly when she arrived at her office late that night.

The card read: "I miss you already."

"Your South Dakota fella has more class than the average cowboy," Bert observed, leaning against her open door.

"How do you know how much class cowboys have? And he's not my fella."

"Sorry," Bert said, entering the office to make peace. "I should have known you'd be tired after the long flight. I told the lawyers we'd meet them for a drink at Provolone in an hour. That gives you time to make a phone call."

Carly read the card again and softened toward Bert. "I didn't mean to snap at you. I'm wishing I hadn't left. We left a lot of things hanging."

"So call him."

"I shouldn't."

"You're nervous, aren't you?"

"Scared to death," Carly admitted.

"That's nonsense," Bert said brusquely. "Call him and talk. Your motto has always been to go after something if you want it, Carly."

Bert was right, she knew. He left her office, and she was already dialing an operator. In a moment she was transferred to the information service and was promptly stymied.

"There's no Hank Fowler at that address," the operator said calmly.

"Try Henry Fowler," Carly suggested, absently rustling through the stack of mail that had accumulated on her desk during her trip.

The operator came back on the line an instant later. "I'm sorry."

Puzzled, Carly said, "What about Becky Fowler?"

The operator punched in the code, and an automated voice promptly recited the correct telephone number for Becky Fowler. Carly wrote it down and immediately dialed the number.

Hank himself picked up the phone on the second ring. "Hello?"

"It's me."

He gave a laugh that made her heart warm. "I had a hunch it might be. Are you all right? Safe flight? Made your connection?"

"I'm fine. I'm here in my office getting ready for a meeting."

"So late?"

"It's one of those things," she said, sinking into her swivel chair. She hugged herself, and murmured, "I'd rather be with you."

"I wish you were. We've got to see each other again, Carly." His voice deepened. "Soon."

Smiling at the intimacy of his tone, Carly said, "I can't get away until the weekend."

"I was thinking I might come to you."

She sat up straight, tingling with excitement. "You're serious!"

"Absolutely," he said with calm. "I can't get you out of my head. As soon as your photographer friend is finished, I'll be on a plane."

"Oh, Hank, that would be wonderful. Did Alexis arrive yet?"

"This afternoon with her entourage." Hank was laughing at the memory. "She's threatening to get us all up before dawn to take advantage of the sunrise. She took some preliminary shots, as she called them. I don't think they're what you're expecting, Carly—"

"I trust Alexis completely," she said, delighted that her plans were progressing so smoothly. "Do everything she says, and you'll be finished in no time."

"Well—"

"Really, she's the best."

"Yes, ma'am."

"And Hank," she added, "tell Becky I'll send her the check in the morning."

"Thanks, love." His voice sounded sincere. "It will make a big difference around here."

A long silence followed, and Carly closed her eyes

to savor the moment. She tried to imagine what Hank might be looking like at that moment. Longingly, she sighed.

"I know," Hank murmured softly. "I feel the same way."

I love you, Carly wanted to say. The words almost popped out of her mouth. But she held them inside, sure that it was too soon.

Besides, this might be a short-term fling. Hot sex and nothing else, right?

Another inner voice said more insistently, *This is the real thing, Carly.*

Into the pause, Hank said, "You'll be glad to know that Baby's fine. Eating her head off."

A smile tugged at Carly's mouth. "Do I detect a note of fondness in your voice at last? Has Baby finally made a friend out of you?"

"She bit Chet today." Hank began to laugh. "Made him bleed, too. I love her!"

"She didn't! Oh, poor Chet!"

"He'll live. And so will she, by the way. The vet stopped by this afternoon and took a peek at her. He says we should be able to turn her loose after he's had a chance to observe her for rabies."

"Thank you for taking care of her."

"I'd rather be taking care of you."

"That sounds nice."

"Carly?"

But Carly looked up as Bert tapped on her office door at that moment. Pulling on his trendy beige jacket, her partner pointed at his watch. She nodded in comprehension. It was nearly time to leave for their meeting.

Into the phone, she said, "Listen, I've got to run. We'll talk again soon."

"When?"

"Tomorrow. Say, did you know the phone number is listed in your sister's name?"

"What?" He sounded blank.

"I didn't bother bringing my book to the office, so I had to call information for your phone number. It's listed in Becky's name."

"I can explain," he said swiftly, "but not when you're in a rush."

"Oh! Did I thank you for the flowers? They're beautiful."

"I'm glad they arrived. I really do miss you, Carly." He knew she was in a hurry and managed to say only, "You're something special. I don't want to lose you."

Yes, yes, yes! She nearly shrieked with joy.

"We'll work something out," she promised, getting to her feet. "I know we will. But now I have to run. We'll talk tomorrow."

"Right."

Another silence ensued—this one laden with words neither was ready to say just yet. Carly laughed unsteadily and said, "Bye."

Hank said, "Bye."

As she cradled the phone, Bert blew the mood. "Shake a leg, Carly. We're going to be late!"

The following day turned into a nightmare of meetings for Carly, but she felt good about settling the copyright problem with a minimum of fuss and no extra legal fees for Twilight Calendars. By cell phone on the way back from the airport where she'd seen off the New York contingent, she informed Bert of their victory.

"Wonderful," Bert crowed. "Come back to the office for a drink."

"I'd rather just go home, if you don't mind, Bert. I'm tired and I have some calls to make." *One in particular,* she almost added.

Bert wheedled, "Alexis sent some photos by modem from her laptop. Don't you want a sneak peek of your cowboy without his shirt?"

Carly was surprised, but delighted. "He took his shirt off for her?"

"And looks pretty good, I must say. But if you'd rather go home—"

In a heartbeat, Carly changed her plans. "I'll be there in half an hour."

Bert laughed. "I'll keep the home fires burning until you get here."

Carly changed her route, and the freeway cooperated for once. She got back to the office in short order.

She found Bert in his office with the photos called up on his computer. He stood up and spun his chair around for Carly to take so she could view the pictures Alexis had sent.

"Are they any good?" she asked, out of breath as she took the chair Bert offered.

"Very good," Bert replied, leaning down to view the screen with her. "A few minutes ago Alexis sent the stuff she shot today, and it's even better than what came back earlier. See?"

Carly stared at the computer screen and could not

understand what was staring back at her. "I don't get it," she said. "These pictures aren't Hank."

"What?"

"They're Chet!"

"Who's Chet?"

Totally baffled, Carly pointed one shaking finger at the small computer screen. "Him! That's not Hank at all. Where's Hank?"

"Wait a minute. These pictures are just right for the calendar." Bert bent closer to the computer and pointed with a pencil. "This guy's a perfect cowboy. Look at that horse! And the sunrise is wonderful! See how Alexis picked up the color of his hair in the trees?"

"But it's not Hank!" Carly exploded. She pounded her fist on the desk. "Where is he?"

"Who cares? This guy is great!"

"I want Hank!" Carly cried.

"But Carly—"

"How could Alexis make such a mistake? She photographed the wrong man! Give me the telephone!"

"But—!"

Bert gave up as Carly grabbed his telephone and fumbled for her book and the Fowler phone number. In less than a minute, she was talking to Becky, who sounded very sleepy.

"Is Hank there? I'd like to speak with him."

"Wha— What time is it? Lord, it's after midnight!"

"I'm sorry, Becky. I didn't think of the time zones. Can I talk to Hank?"

"Who is this?"

"Carly. Carly Cortazzo, remember? I'd like to speak with Hank."

"Oh! Carly." Becky yawned. "He left earlier today. Henry's not here."

"Where is he?"

"He left." Becky was half-asleep and not very helpful. "Do you know what time it is?"

"Yes, yes, I'm sorry I—look, what about Alexis? Is she nearby?"

Becky mumbled something and dropped the phone. For an instant, Carly feared she had fallen back to sleep, but a moment later the sound of a door slamming and more voices eased her concern. Carly drummed her fingers on Bert's desk. A few minutes passed before the unmistakably laconic voice that belonged to Alexis Carmichael came on the line.

"Hi-ya, Carly. How'd you like my switcheroo? Aren't the pictures fantastic?"

"Lexie, what's going on? Where is Hank?"

"Beats me, honey. We had a big laugh this morning, and he took off. I spent the day with Chet. Isn't he yummy? I wish he wasn't engaged to Becky."

"But—I don't understand. Hank is supposed to be our cowboy."

Alexis sounded amused. "Honey, if you thought Henry Fowler was a real cowboy, I've got a bridge in Brooklyn that's for sale. He's a hunk, but not exactly Wild Bill Hickok."

"What do you mean?"

"I figured you wanted an authentic man of the wide-open spaces, so we voted Chet for the job."

"Who's we?"

"Henry and me. He's a neat guy, but hardly material for Twilight. I like him."

Carly still didn't understand what was happening. "Why isn't he material for Twilight?"

"Because his IQ is bigger than his bicep measurement," Alexis said blandly. "He's got brains— and a body that's not bad, but hardly what I usually see on your pages. You like the baby-oil look, right?"

"But—"

"Are you disappointed?" Alexis asked.

Carly tried to collect her wits. "I…I just don't understand, Lexie. Hank's the real thing, isn't he?"

"You've been looking at the wrong kind of man, honey, if you had Henry pegged for a cowpoke. How do you like the photos of Chet? Carly? Are you there?"

Carly gave up trying to make sense of it all and handed the telephone to Bert. She got up from the chair and walked to the wide windows that overlooked L.A. There, she leaned her forehead against the glass. Her mind was spinning. Her heart was seething.

Why would he lie?

Mentally, she tried to review every word she'd ever spoken to Hank and every sentence he'd replied. He *had* ridden horses. She remembered the first moment she saw him—galloping along the horizon on the black stallion. And his roping skills—surely a man couldn't fake that?

And yet he'd been a klutz at just about everything else around the ranch. What had Chet said about Hank and horses? Carly couldn't remember. He'd avoided taking her for a ride, though, instead encouraging Carly to walk to the hilltop overlooking the ranch.

With a blush, Carly realized they'd probably spent more time making love than anything else. She hadn't enjoyed many opportunities to see Hank in action around the ranch. Except in bed.

The same question kept swirling in her mind. *Why would he lie?*

The land means something to me, he'd said. *It's where my family belongs, and I'm ready to do anything to make sure things stay that way.*

But later he'd said, *Becky's the important factor.*

That had to be it. *Becky* had entered the contest. It was Becky who needed the money. Hank had just gone along with the scheme so his sister could keep the ranch.

"That explains why the phone is in her name," Carly said aloud.

Bert had finished speaking with Alexis and hung up the receiver. "What about the phone?"

Carly turned around, breathing raggedly. "I've been had, Bert."

He grinned. "Did you enjoy it?"

"That's not what I— Oh, hell! I can't think!" She gripped her head and began to pace the office carpet. "I don't know what's going on!"

"Well, Alexis has some great photographs for us, and I think the next calendar's going to be a success." Bert settled on the edge of his desk. "You got a vacation, some great sex and everyone's happy. What else matters?"

"You don't understand!" Carly cried.

"What's not to understand? All's right with the world, as far as I can see."

"But I was falling in love with him!" Carly cried. "And he was lying to me! The whole time, he was lying."

"About what, exactly?"

"Everything!"

"Really everything?" Bert pressed affectionately. "Or only a few things?"

Carly shook her head wildly. "I don't know."

"About falling in love with you?"

"He never said he was," she replied, fighting hard to keep her voice steady. "If he had, then I probably would hate him right now."

"Then it's a good thing he didn't tell you how he was feeling. Why don't you talk to him?"

"I don't know where he is."

"Ah," said Bert, nodding. "That's a problem."

"He's going to show up, though," Carly said with certainty. She began to pull herself together firmly. "And when he does get here…he'd better be prepared!"

Henry took the last flight into Los Angeles and arrived in the city at six in the morning. The airport was practically deserted at that hour, except for a few noisy travelers headed home from Las Vegas. Henry enjoyed their high spirits, and he found himself smiling as he arrived at the rental car counter. A car was easily procured, and he headed for the nearest hotel to sleep and clean up.

Midafternoon, he telephoned Twilight Calendars

and reached Carly at last. The impact of hearing her voice again caused his heart to accelerate.

"Hi," she said, sounding breathless as she came on the line. "Where are you?"

"In L.A. At the Fairfax. I have a meeting in town at four. I'll be finished by seven."

"What kind of meeting? Are you buying more cows for the old homestead?" Her tone was teasing.

"Not exactly. I'll tell you all about it over dinner. Carly—"

"Great!" Her voice was happy—almost jaunty. "There's a place that's just perfect for a cowpoke like you only a short drive from that hotel. I'll come for you at the Fairfax at seven. And Hank?"

"Yes?"

"Wear your spurs."

She laughed and cradled the phone before he could make a comeback, so Henry hung up feeling odd. Spurs?

At four, he met the woman who would be representing him in negotiations with the Los Angeles paper. They spoke briefly, then presented themselves at the headquarters of one of the nation's largest and most widely circulated newspapers. They were whisked into a posh suite and offered several kinds of bottled water before sitting down to talk turkey with the committee that hoped to franchise the Henry Fowler column.

Henry listened to their pitch, then tossed out the ideas that had been percolating in his head. Clearly, he described his plan for combining adventure and recreation with his particular critical opinions. At first, they couldn't grasp his concept at all.

Then the marketing manager snapped his fingers. "I've got it! Indiana Jones!"

"No, no—"

One of the editors chimed in. "Hey, great idea!"

"That's not exactly what I meant. Let me try explaining it this way—"

"We could photograph you in a fedora and put it on every bus in every city up and down the coast!"

"Hold on—"

"We'll give you a generous travel budget."

They all chimed in enthusiastically.

"And a salary with complete benefits and four weeks' vacation. Plus our top-notch retirement plan, investment opportunities and tickets to the Academy Awards!"

Henry sank back in his seat and looked over at Margie Williams, his agent. She nodded and leaned forward to take charge of the meeting. "First of all, Henry wants complete authority over any marketing plans you may devise. As for salary…"

Henry listened while Margie outlined the terms under which he would agree to write for the newspaper syndicate. She was calm and tough, asking for more than Henry would have if left to his own devices. He was surprised when all the terms were accepted.

"Well, then," said Margie, turning to Henry. "Then it's up to Mr. Fowler. What do you say, Henry?"

He did not hesitate. "I'll think about everything overnight and get back to you tomorrow."

Everyone around the table seemed pleased. Henry left Margie and walked back to his hotel in the late-afternoon heat, his head swimming with the possibilities. In his heart he knew he wanted the new job. Reorganizing his life was the tricky part.

His home and friends were in Seattle, but he didn't have to live there if something better turned up. Now he had the whole West Coast to roam. From Santa Fe to Vancouver, he could go wherever he pleased. Perhaps it was time to renew his pilot's license, he thought with pleasure. There was no need to tie himself to the condo in Seattle anymore.

He hadn't expected his life to change so much, but suddenly Henry felt as if he were standing at the top of a very long and exciting ski slope.

He wanted to share the great news and bought flowers for Carly in the hotel boutique. He needed her opinion and longed to hear her thoughts. More than anything, he wanted to be with Carly again.

Suddenly he heard her voice behind him in the lobby. Hank turned around, ready to call her name.

It was Carly, all right. But for an instant, Hank didn't recognize her. She strode into the lobby wearing a ridiculous cowboy getup complete with rhinestones on her shirt and fringe on her buckskin shirt. She wore snakeskin boots on her feet and a cocky white Stetson-style hat atop her blond hair. Her earrings were gold pistols, and from her shoulder swung a bag in the shape of a miniature Spanish saddle. Dolly Parton never looked half so silly.

"C—Carly?"

She swung around and laughed. "Howdy, Hank! How are you, sugar pie?"

Hank staggered backward as she flung her arms around his neck and planted a huge, red-lipsticked kiss on his mouth. Someone laughed from the direction of the reception desk. He almost dropped the flowers he was holding in one hand, but his other arm automatically went around her slim body.

She feels like Carly, he thought dimly. *She just doesn't look like her.*

Carly pulled back and looked up at him with devilment sparkling in her blue eyes. "What's the matter, Hank? You look surprised to see me."

Almost too astonished to speak, he asked, "What in the world is going on?"

"Why, I'm taking you out on the town, that's all. C'mon! The limo's waiting."

"Limo?" Hank's head spun in confusion.

Laughing, Carly dragged him by the hand until they were outside the hotel. There, parked at the end of the canopy, stood the most ridiculous limousine Hank had ever seen in his life. It was painted white with big brown cow spots. The roof had been replaced by a gigantic cowboy hat, and an enormous rack of horns from a steer. The driver blew the horn, and the air was torn by the bellow of an enraged bull.

The hotel doorman looked as if a real cow had suddenly made an unsanitary deposit on the immaculate carpet.

"What do you think?" Carly asked. "Does it make you feel like home?"

Hank recovered enough poise to say, "I think I'm catching on now. Carly, if this is your way of—"

"My way of making you feel welcome in Los Angeles. It is, sugar pie. Now, hop in. I've got another surprise in store for you!"

Hank couldn't resist her and allowed Carly to drag

him into the back seat of the long car. Once the door was closed, he remembered the flowers and handed them into her lap.

"Here," he said. "I know these are a small apology for everything I've done, but—"

"Roses! Aren't they beautiful." Carly held the fragrant bouquet to her nose and managed to knock off her cowboy hat. "Oops. I can't lose this, can I?"

Hank took the hat from her hand and tossed it on the opposite seat as the limousine began to move. He decided to make his move, too, and wound his arms around Carly. Pressing her back into the cushions, he swooped in to kiss her.

Carly didn't resist, but wrapped her arms around his neck. She met the coming kiss eagerly, her lips full of fire.

Any worries Hank entertained that Carly might be truly angry with him evaporated with that kiss. She was still Carly—the woman who had cried and laughed in his arms, made steamy love with him and watched Hank make a fool of himself back in South Dakota. He thought he could feel her heart tremble beneath all those rhinestones, and when he touched her knee with his fingertips, he absorbed her quiver.

When he withdrew only far enough to press softer kisses against her earlobe, Hank whispered, "I've missed you. It feels like we've been apart for ages."

"I'm glad you came," Carly whispered back, then slid her unsteady fingers into his hair to draw Hank's lips to her own again.

Hank savored the taste of her, the scent of her skin, the silky texture of her hair. She felt exciting in his arms, full of promise and surprises.

"Carly, where are we going?"

Her eyes sparkled up at him. "The perfect place for dinner."

"Can I convince you to turn this crazy limo around and go back to my hotel?"

"And miss all the fun I have planned for you? Not on your neckerchief, sweetie. Speaking of neckerchiefs, where is yours?" She tugged at the collar of his cashmere shirt, feigning surprise at finding him dressed so differently. "And your boots? And those nice dusty jeans?"

"I know I've got some explaining to do."

Carly touched his lips with her forefinger. "Not until after we've painted the town, Hank. Ready? Here's where we'll work up our appetites."

Hank looked out the car window and found that the driver had brought them to a country-western bar complete with a cactus and a horse tied up out front.

The horse was real, too. It stood placidly in front of a hitching post. The name of the bar flashed in neon, "Monty's Midnight Saloon."

Hank said, "Oh, no."

Laughing, Carly climbed over him and popped open the car door. "Let's go, cowboy! I want you to show all these city slickers some of your fancy bronc-busting."

Hank groaned. "Carly, what have you done?"

She skipped up the sidewalk to the door of the bar and patted the nose of the tied horse. "This sweetheart reminds me of Laverne, don't you think?"

Without waiting for his response, she tipped her hat at the establishment's bouncer, who was dressed like a rodeo rider except that he wasn't wearing a shirt. His arms bulged with muscles, and his hair was perfectly blown dry. The young man towered over Hank and looked as if he might outweigh both Carly and Hank put together.

"Hi, Delbert," Carly said gaily. "Did you save us some space on the dance floor?"

"Oh, there's plenty of room inside, Miss Cortazzo," replied the young man, with a trace of shyness in his smile. He opened the door for them. "Monty's doesn't really get busy until later."

"Maybe we'll stay all night!" she cried, sashaying through the teepee-shaped doorway of Monty's Midnight Saloon.

"Who was that?" Hank asked, momentarily blinded when they plunged into a dazzling display of flashing disco lights.

"One of Twilight's former models. Isn't he sweet? Delbert was in our pet-look-alike calendar."

"What was his pet? An elephant?"

"No, a rottweiler puppy. They were adorable together. How about a drink?"

Hank followed Carly into the nightspot, taking notice of the neon lights shaped like bucking broncos and howling coyotes. Wailing country music rent the air. A few brightly clad patrons were dancing on a shiny floor strewn with peanut shells. Delbert was right. There was plenty of room inside.

The waitresses who circulated among the small tables were dressed in Native American costumes, but Hank didn't recognize the tribe. He doubted that any self-respecting Sioux could have survived a single winter in such short skirts.

The bartender was a John Wayne look-alike. He

leaned down and said in a Duke-like drawl, "Howdy, pilgrims. Are you parched?"

"What?"

Carly nudged Hank with her elbow. "He wants to know if we'd like a drink."

"Oh, sure. Uh—what's the specialty of the house?"

"Tonight it's margaritas."

Hank gulped. "Well, when in Rome."

John Wayne leaned his elbow on the bar and stuck his face close to Hank's. "This ain't Rome, pilgrim. It's Monty's Midnight Saloon. And if you don't want a drink, you can hightail it outta here."

"Okay, okay." Hank put some cash on the bar. "We'll take two."

"Let's dance!" Carly cried as the bartender turned away to prepare their drinks.

"Carly—"

"Do you know how to two-step?"

"I'll fake it."

Hank was pleased to see the surprise on Carly's face when he seized her around the waist and steered her onto the dance floor in a moderately serviceable two-step. He spun her twice, making her laugh. The music must have been loud enough to rival a live rock concert, but the dancers seemed to enjoy the howls of the singer.

But halfway around the floor, Carly spied the mechanical bull whirling riderlessly in one corner. "Ohh, look!" she cried. "Why don't you show us how it's done, Hank?"

"You want to see me killed?"

"Believe me," she retorted, "I've considered

murdering you myself for the past day or so. Come on, get up on that bull, cowboy!''

"I think you've had your fun,'' said Hank, pulling her back into the dance.

Carly managed to blink up at him. "What do you mean?"

"I can see you've figured out the whole thing.''

"I have?''

"Look, I never meant for the charade to get out of hand,'' Hank said sincerely. "Everything I did was wrong, I know.''

"Then why did you do it?''

He spread his hands helplessly. "I don't know. It seemed right at the time.''

"And now?''

Surprised, Hank realized that Carly had tears in her eyes. This was the last thing he expected to find—himself tongue-tied and Carly upset. He said, "I didn't think it would be important.''

"The truth isn't important?'' Her gaze began to flash even hotter than before.

"Not always, no. I knew you'd come to South Dakota with a plan to take a lot of stupid pictures. In a few days, you'd leave. What could a little white lie hurt?''

Carly's cheeks flushed. "Stupid pictures? It's my career, you know!''

"That's not what I— Hey, don't get bent out of shape over this, Carly. It's not— Wait! Carly!''

She turned away from him and started walking.

Hank started after her.

But John Wayne grabbed his arm and spun Hank

around. "Hey, pilgrim," the bartender rasped. "Are you hassling that little lady?"

"Of course not!"

"'Cause we don't take kindly to fellers who don't drink their margaritas and then go picking on pretty ladies."

Nine

Carly stormed out into the night air and headed straight for the limousine. She was insane, she knew. Walking away from Hank wasn't what she wanted at all. But she couldn't stop herself. A wildly crazy woman had taken over inside her. She got into the car and slammed the door.

"Get me out of here."

As the car pulled away from the curb, she glanced around and saw Hank running out of Monty's.

Hank skidded to a stop on the sidewalk and shouted, "Carly, come back here!"

But the car smoothly accelerated away from the curb, and Carly couldn't summon her voice to stop it.

Hank stared after the limo, stunned at finding himself alone.

From the doorway, Delbert said, "Looks like she dumped you, pal."

"I can't believe it." Hank couldn't tear his eyes from the disappearing limo.

"That Miss Cortazzo," said Delbert, shaking his head, "she's got a temper."

"I've got to go after her," Hank said to himself, then swung on Delbert. "Can you call me a cab?"

The bouncer shrugged. "Sure, but it'll take ten minutes to get here."

Hank cursed. "I can't let her go."

"Sorry, pal, but it's the best I can do."

Hank could *not* let Carly escape. Not today. Without a second thought, he headed straight for the buckskin horse that had been tied up outside Monty's Midnight Saloon. He grabbed the reins and began unwrapping them from the hitching post. The animal woke up from its nap and snorted.

"Hey!" Delbert shouted. "What d'you think you're doing?"

"I'll bring him back," Hank promised, turning the horse around on the sidewalk.

"That's Monty's horse," Delbert objected, stepping into Hank's path. "That's Rocky! You can't take Rocky!"

"My apologies to Monty," Hank shot back, one foot already in the stirrup.

Swinging aboard Rocky's splendidly decorated saddle, Hank planted his other foot squarely in Delbert's chest and pushed. Delbert gave a surprised "oof!" and fell back on the sidewalk. Rocky chose that moment to rear back on his hind legs, nearly dumping Hank into the cactus bed.

But Hank hung on. For dear life. He seized a handful of Rocky's mane and kept his balance. Then Rocky jolted down on all four feet, gave a happy little buck and bolted into the street, sending cars scattering in all directions.

"Whoa!" Hank cried automatically. "What is this? A prison break? Whoa!"

But the sight of Carly's limousine disappearing around the next corner made Hank throw caution to the wind.

"Hey, Rocky!" he shouted. "Show me what you've got!"

Rocky did. Apparently his long nap in front of Monty's had left him completely refreshed and rarin' to go. Like a race horse shooting out of the starting gate, he put his head down and broke into a gallop straight up Sunset Boulevard. Car brakes squealed, drivers shouted, a busload of tourists hung out the windows of their bus and snapped pictures. Hank barely controlled a scream of terror.

But Rocky was a demon. His strides lengthened, his hooves struck sparks on the pavement. He tore up the street past restaurants and ice cream vendors. He galloped past a convertible filled with astonished teenagers.

Hank stayed in the saddle by some miracle. In seconds he was whizzing down the street, barely conscious of anything but the flying horse. He saw a police car flash by, then palm trees, a man selling maps to movie stars' homes and two bikers with their Harleys. But mainly he clung to Rocky's plunging neck and tried to see Carly's limousine through the horse's flying mane.

He reined Rocky around the corner where he'd last seen Carly disappear, then spotted the limo at the next light. When he gave Rocky his head again, the horse bolted ahead as if stung by a swarm of angry bees.

The light changed. The limo moved forward. Hank shouted. Rocky galloped.

The limo turned right, and Hank thought he caught a glimpse of Carly's astonished face looking out at him from the back seat. He tried to turn Rocky, but the horse was moving too fast. The buckskin nearly ran down a bicyclist, who screamed and rode straight into a flower bed.

But the limo slowed down! It stopped!

Rocky spun on his powerful haunches, took two strides and gathered himself, then leaped over an in-line skater who was bent over to fasten his skates. He landed back on the sidewalk. Hank nearly somersaulted over Rocky's head, but kept his seat. A dog-walking pedestrian shrieked and dodged out of their way.

With fresh speed, Rocky headed straight for the limousine. Three, four, five strides and he was almost on top of the car. Hank barely had enough strength to haul back on the reins in time to keep Rocky from jumping right over the limo. With just inches to spare, Rocky jammed to a stop.

And suddenly Hank was airborne.

The world seemed to turn into slow motion. Like a graceful bird, Hank soared through the air. He wanted to yelp, but there was no time. He thought he heard Carly scream.

He hit the roof of the limo, tumbled head over

heels and thumped his head going through the sun-roof.

The next thing he knew, Hank was sprawled inside the limousine, stunned and staring up at Carly.

"Oh, Hank, are you all right? Are you hurt? Talk to me, please! Should we take you to a hospital?"

"Llurph," he managed to say, still dizzy from the impact.

Carly scrambled down next to him on the floor of the car. She cradled his head gently in her lap, her face close to his and looking frightened. "What, darling? What did you say?"

"I lurph," he mumbled.

Carly cried out. "Oh, God! Driver! Where's the nearest hospital?"

But Hank caught Carly's hand at last and looked up into her beautiful, worried face. He shook his head and said quite clearly this time, "I love you."

Carly stared down at him. "You do?"

"You think I'd ride a horse up Sunset Boulevard for anything less?"

"Oh, Hank! I was coming back around the block to get you at Monty's. I love you, too. I love you even if you can't ride a horse!"

He forced himself to sit up beside her, moving gingerly. "I thought I did pretty well this time."

"You did, you did." Carly helped him to the seat of the car and called to the driver, "Will you please catch that horse for us? He might get hurt in all this traffic."

The driver was already out of the limo and managed to grab Rocky's trailing reins. There was no need to worry about the horse dashing into traffic, however. A large crowd of tourists had surrounded him and lavished the puffing buckskin with attention.

A baseball-capped tourist stuck his head inside the open driver's door. "Hey, mister? Are you a stunt rider for that new Western movie?"

Another head appeared. "Yeah, that stunt was great! Can we take your picture?"

Carly and Hank collapsed with laughter and ended up kissing on the back seat.

"Come on," Carly whispered a few minutes later. "Let's take the horse back and then go to my condo."

They extricated Rocky from his fan club and set off on foot, leading the horse back to Monty's Midnight Saloon. The limousine followed, creating an odd-looking parade as the evening light waned.

By ten o'clock they arrived at Carly's home, a modern condominium on a hillside overlooking the sparkling lights of the city. They waved goodbye to the limousine driver, then crossed the patio and went inside, carrying bags of takeout food they'd picked up at Monty's.

Hank wasn't sure what to expect as he entered Carly's home. Her foyer and living room were sleekly designed, with high ceilings and lots of windows. The spare furnishings glowed with simple but vivid colors, reflecting the taste of a woman with an artistic eye.

A geometric quilt decorated one wall, a pair of seascapes another. Her travel experiences were remembered in the grouping of objects on a low coffee table—some rustic pottery, a stack of picture books about Italy, a bonsai tree in a jade green pot.

A baby grand piano stood in an alcove as if waiting for a concert pianist to show up and entertain a party of elegant and sophisticated guests.

Approaching the piano, Hank twinkled the keys, and asked, "Do you play?"

"Not well, despite all the lessons I took as a kid." She smiled, watching Hank get accustomed to her home. "It's my father's. I keep it here because there's no room in his apartment."

She carried the food into her kitchen, leaving Hank to savor the mental picture of a very young Carly diligently practicing her piano lessons.

He strolled to the kitchen doorway and enfolded Carly in his arms when she came out. "I look forward to getting to know everything about you."

She melted against his body and looped her arms around his neck. "I'm the one looking forward to the truth."

"I have a lot of explaining to do," he admitted.

"I gather you aren't a rancher in South Dakota?" Carly lifted her eyebrows.

"No." He stroked her cheek with his fingertips. "This is strange, isn't it? You don't even know who I am."

"I've been trying to guess."

Carly led him to the rear of the house, past a darkened bedroom to another small niche. She flipped on a small, glowing lamp. Beneath a large, arched window that overlooked the city stood a deeply cushioned sofa—obviously the place Carly liked best in her house. A filled bookshelf, a telephone and fax machine, an armoire that clearly hid a television set—all the comforts a busy single woman could wish for in a retreat. Her bedroom lay just a few yards away.

Carly was glad to have Hank in her home. It felt right to see him among her things. She pulled him down onto the sofa. Ready to hear everything, she tucked her feet up and leaned into his arm.

Hank took a deep breath and took the plunge. "I'm a writer for a newspaper. Or newspapers, I guess. I live in Seattle."

"Seattle?" Carly felt a pang of fear. "That's so far away."

"I write a column that involves travel and politics," he continued. And thereafter he explained his career to her.

His life sounded exciting, stimulating and hectic. Carly was familiar with his column in a distant sort of way. It was not carried by any of the newspapers she read on a daily or weekly basis, but she realized she must have read some of his work while she traveled. Hank's writing was the kind that had a great future.

She smiled, glad that he was accomplished and respected in his field. She longed to hear more about his column, and looked forward to the many conversations they would have.

If they had a future together.

"Anyway," Hank concluded after a few minutes, "I don't live in South Dakota. Becky owns the ranch, lock, stock and barrel. She's the one who runs it."

"You rarely go there?"

"Hardly ever."

"And Becky's in some kind of financial trouble."

"Right. She heard about your calendar contest and

decided it was a great way to make her mortgage payments. Trouble was, your contest specified cowboy and she didn't fit the bill.''

"So she sent your pictures instead."

"Yes." Ruefully, Hank added, "I had no idea what she'd done until you were on your way to take my picture."

"But since she needed the money, you agreed to do the calendar."

"Yes. We didn't see the need to tell you the truth. What did it matter whether I was the genuine article or not? I was a face you needed, that's it. But I couldn't go through with the plan, Carly. Not after you and I, well, it was that first night on the porch, I suppose."

"What do you mean?"

"Until then, I hadn't realized you'd be a real person. It was easier when you were just a corporate entity. But I liked Carly Cortazzo." He touched her face again, bringing a lump to Carly's throat. "You were a pretty tough broad on the outside, but I saw someone I could really care about on the inside."

"You could have been honest with me from the start."

"I wasn't sure about that."

Carly swallowed hard and tried to explain. "Maybe it *was* important at first for you to be a cowboy. I...I had this silly fantasy in my head—"

"A fantasy?"

"Yes, about you and—and—well, it seemed important that you were a man of the wide-open spaces. In my head you came from a simpler time, I guess.

It...it felt more romantic, somehow. There's something about a cowboy.''

"What, exactly?''

"I can't explain it. I suppose I wanted to be swept off my feet by a man who rode the range and sang to his cattle and did all that cowboy stuff.''

Hank laughed, drawing Carly closer. ''I've never sung a single note to a cow in my life, and I don't care if I ever set eyes on a horse again. But,'' he added, his voice deepening, ''I *can* sweep you off your feet, Carly.''

She lifted her mouth to his and let Hank press a long and delicious kiss into her soul. Her heart beat erratically in her chest, making Carly breathless. His mouth was warm, but it was the warmth that emanated from within Hank that made Carly feel toasty inside.

But a giggle started to bubble in her throat, and soon she was shaking with amusement.

Hank pulled back and looked at her quizzically. ''Have I lost my ability to make your head swim?''

"No,'' she said, trying to smother her laughter with her hand. ''Not at all. I was just thinking about my first glimpse of you—riding that black horse right up to me on the road. And you jumped off!''

"No, I fell,'' Hank admitted.

"And you fell off again the next day when we were looking for strays?'' The mental picture appeared to her, and Carly couldn't stop the fresh flood of giggles.

"I have no idea how to look for strays,'' Hank replied quite honestly. ''That day I was doing my best not to get killed.''

Laughing aloud at last, Carly asked, "And...and what about roping that steer? It dragged you through the bushes and— Oh, I've never seen anyone look so funny in my life!"

"You didn't think it was funny at the time," he pointed out darkly.

"That's when I didn't know what was really going on! Oh, Hank, you worked so hard to deceive me."

"Do you mind?" he asked, pulling her closer again. A smile tugged at the corners of his mouth. "Are you angry about what Becky and I did?"

Carly shook her head. "You're right. It doesn't matter if you're a cowboy or a famous newspaper writer. I love both of you, even though you'll always be Hank to me."

"And I love you."

"I'm so glad."

"Will you mind if the cowboy never shows his face again?"

Wistfully Carly ran her finger down the line of his jaw. "It's a very nice face. But I guess Chet Roswell's will do for the calendar."

Hank smiled with relief. "Thank you. Believe me, I was dreading the explanation I was going to have to give to my colleagues in Seattle if my likeness showed up on a Twilight Calendar."

"Have you ever *seen* a Twilight Calendar?" she challenged.

"Of course. The women in my office often tack them up on the bulletin board. We had a discussion about sexist behavior, but the men lost. After centuries of oppression, we decided they could have one calendar around."

"I never claimed we were politically correct," Carly said airily. "We're not forcing anyone to buy our calendars."

"But I think you're ready to try something else with your life," Hank guessed.

"Maybe. I can't leave Bert by himself—not yet. But something new might turn up for me if I started looking around a little."

Huskily Hank said, "I want you to be happy, Carly. I want to be the one to make you happy."

"You could make me happy right now," she whispered.

He smiled. "I could?"

Carly stood up. Taking his hand, she pulled Hank to his feet. "Come with me."

He hesitated only for a second. "Are you sure, Carly? Sure that you want me?"

"Very sure."

"My name isn't even Hank, you know."

"Should I call you Henry now?"

He thought it over and shook his head. "I'm getting used to hearing Hank. And I like the way you say it."

"Then Hank it is."

She led the way to her bedroom. A small candle stood on the night table, and Carly lit it with a long-stemmed match. When she turned around, Hank reached for her and began to unfasten the rhinestone buttons on her shirt.

Softly he said, "You don't know how much I want to see this thing off you. Where *did* you get this outfit, anyway?"

"It doesn't matter. You'll never see it again."

"Oh, I don't know," he murmured, smiling and softly kissing her bare shoulder as the tacky shirt came off. "It's kind of kinky."

Carly laughed, but her voice trembled with anticipation. Hank's lips were hot on her skin. His hands were expert in stripping off her clothing, piece by piece.

With shaking hands, Carly dropped each item of Hank's clothing on the floor, too. She knew his body so well that a few short caresses made his voice go hoarse.

"I've missed you, Carly."

"We've barely been apart a day."

"Even a day is too long."

Carly pushed the lacy bedclothes back and pulled Hank down onto her bed. The softness enveloped them, feeling, oh, so much more comfortable than the rough South Dakota ground.

Lips against her skin, Hank murmured, "I always want to be this close to you, Carly."

Carly settled beneath him and wrapped her arms around Hank's shoulders. She whispered, "We can be even closer."

"Like this?"

He was inside her then, gently pressing Carly down into the bed with an achingly gentle force that took her breath so sharply that tears sprang to her eyes. She closed them, the better to experience every sensation Hank evoked in her. He was hers, she thought. Completely her own.

And she wanted to be just as completely his, she realized, arching upward to pull him deeply within herself. Each thrust seemed to fill Carly with joy as well as pleasure. She could feel the burning imprints his fingertips seemed to leave on her breasts, her thighs, as if they seared his name into her receiving flesh.

They rolled together, and then Carly was over him, unwilling to be separated for an instant, but obeying his demands. She reveled in the touch of his hands. He took her nipples into his mouth and teased her to the brink of implosion with his tongue. She gasped.

All conscious thought eluded Carly as he coaxed her body to even more delicious heights. All her senses spun with love. She was hardly aware when Hank pushed her down onto the bed again, but suddenly he was inside her once more. She wrapped her thighs tightly around his hips.

"Open your eyes," he breathed. "I want you totally, Carly, love."

She obeyed instinctively and found herself drowning in the emotion that radiated from Hank. He thrust within her, slowly at first, then with an even-more-passionate tempo, driving Carly deeper and deeper into a vortex of sensual darkness.

She felt herself turning to liquid, hot and volcanic. Her flesh melded to his, just as their hearts seemed to meld into something all-powerful. Each thrust drew them tighter and tighter, deeper and blacker.

Carly cried out. The vortex drowned her and burst into flame at the same time, firing their two souls into one.

For a long, suspended heartbeat, they clung together, quivering with heat and joy. The rest of the universe ceased to exist. Carly's world was Hank alone.

Later Hank brought her back to the world by stroking her face, murmuring softly, "Are you all right?"

"Of course. Just— Yes, I'm fine."

"I love you."

The words had never sounded so beautiful. "I love you," she replied. "I want to be with you."

"We can be."

"I mean every day, every night."

"I want that, too," Hank said against her temple. "We're going to have to marry, Carly, that's all there is to it."

"Marry?"

"Does that frighten you?"

"No," Carly said, knowing it was true. Her heart swelled. "That's what I want, too, Hank. I want everything."

"Kids? A house? A dog and picket fence?" He was smiling.

"The whole works. After I help Bert get things settled at Twilight."

"And a honeymoon?"

"Naturally. Someplace civilized, please. No camping trips."

Hank shuddered. "Heaven forbid."

Six weeks later Hank found himself reclining in absolute comfort in a rustic wooden chair with his feet up, eyes closed and the last of the summer sun warming his whole body.

Trouble was, he was listening to the mooing of cattle.

The noise made him smile. Then he sensed rather

than saw Carly as she leaned over his prone body and pressed a soft kiss on his forehead.

He mumbled, "I can't believe we came all the way to Italy to listen to cows."

"It's an Italian cattle drive," she reported. "I was just talking to our landlady. She says the farmers are driving their cattle to market today."

Hank opened one eye and looked fondly at his wife. She looked beautifully relaxed—blond hair covered with a chic straw hat, her slim body loosely draped in a light summer dress that showed off the golden glow of her shoulders. There wasn't a rhinestone in sight.

She sat down on his footstool, leaned close and draped one arm around his hips. "If we're lucky, the landlady will buy one perfect cow and we'll have beef for dinner tomorrow."

Hank cocked an eyebrow at her. "Are we staying through tomorrow?"

"While I was downstairs, I used the telephone. I changed our plane reservations. We're staying until next Monday."

Hank opened both eyes to better appreciate the happy glow that seemed to encircle Carly as she sat on the balcony of their room overlooking the piazza of the small Italian village that had been their headquarters for the past week. "Do you have a good reason for changing our plans, my love?"

"Yes. I need more research for the article I'm writing," Carly said. "We'll have to hike up to Mount Aloysius tomorrow so I can take a few photos. Then I thought we'd go across to the lake the next day."

"You're confident this article is going to sell, I presume?"

"I already talked with the paper in Seattle. They're definitely buying. And I think a whole series of articles might make a good book."

"What kind of book?"

"Italy for honeymooners." She took off her hat and tossed it onto the tiles at her feet.

Hank smiled, reaching for her hand. "Sounds like a winner."

"I got the idea from Becky, actually. Her letter suggested she and Chet are looking for a honeymoon trip."

"She'll never leave South Dakota."

"Don't bet the ranch on that, darling."

"Kiss me."

Carly did so warmly, then gently smoothed his hair back from his forehead. Her voice dropped to a murmur. "The rest of the town has gone inside for their siesta."

"Are you suggesting we do the same?"

"In a minute."

Hank stealthily slid one hand up the front of her dress until he encountered the round weight of her breast. He was rewarded by Carly's intimate smile and delicately circled the already erect nipple with his thumb. Beneath her nearly translucent dress, he could see the curve of her belly and the thrust of her slim hip.

One nice thing about Italy, he had observed, was that the neighbors who lounged in their open second-floor windows seemed to encourage public displays of affection. He tugged the strap of her dress off one shoulder.

Carly let him have his way, watching his eyes with love in her gaze. She said, "I've been wondering about the results of all the time we've spent in our honeymoon bed, Hank."

"What results?"

"Well," she said, leaning into his caress of her breast. "What if our children don't care for foreign countries and outdoor cafés, concerts and musty bookshops?"

"You mean—" A disconcerting thought occurred to Hank and made him sit up.

"Yes, what if they like horses and cattle?"

"We'll have to do everything in our power to make sure that doesn't happen."

"Sometimes these things are destined."

"Well, then, we may need to rethink the whole children concept," he replied.

"I'm afraid," murmured Carly, leaning close to kiss him again, "it's too late."

"You mean—"

"Yes," said Carly, her mouth against his to deliver the not-so-dreadful news. "My love, I'm already pregnant with our own little cowboy."

* * * * *

DIANA PALMER
ANN MAJOR
SUSAN MALLERY

RETURN TO WHITEHORN

In **April 1998** get ready to catch the bouquet. Join in the excitement as these bestselling authors lead us down the aisle with three heartwarming tales of love and matrimony in Big Sky country.

A very engaged lady is having second thoughts about her intended; a pregnant librarian is wooed by the town bad boy; a cowgirl meets up with her first love. Which Maverick will be the next one to get hitched?

Available in **April 1998**.

Silhouette's beloved **MONTANA MAVERICKS** returns in Special Edition and Harlequin Historicals starting in February 1998, with brand-new stories from your favorite authors.

Round up these great new stories at your favorite retail outlet.

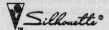

Take 4 bestselling love stories FREE

Plus get a FREE surprise gift!

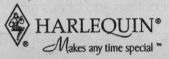

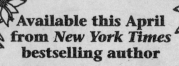

BEVERLY BARTON

**Continues the
twelve-book series—
36 Hours—in April 1998
with Book Ten**

NINE MONTHS

Paige Summers couldn't have been more shocked when she learned that the man with whom she had spent one passionate, stormy night was none other than her arrogant new boss! And just because he was the father of her unborn baby didn't give him the right to claim her as his wife. Especially when he wasn't offering the one thing she wanted: his heart.

For Jared and Paige and *all* the residents of Grand Springs, Colorado, the storm-induced blackout was just the beginning of 36 Hours that changed *everything*! You won't want to miss a single book.

Available at your favorite retail outlet.

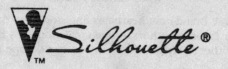

TM